Tabitha

Always a Bridesmaid

Prescott Hill

KARI LEMOR

Rycon Press

TABITHA © 2023 by Kari Lemor

Cover Art by: Karasel Cover Art

First Electronic Edition: May 2023 ISBN - 978-1-954056-25-1

First Print Edition: May 2023 ISBN - 978-1-954056-26-8

Also by Kari Lemor

Sweet and semi-sweet books

Prescott Hill

Donovan
Tabitha

Last Chance Beach

Secrets Under the Sun
Masquerade Under the Moon
Solace Under the Stars

Sounds of Silence

Perfect Silence

Storms of New England

Christmas novellas
Forgotten Dreams
Sweet Dreams

Rangers of Acadia

Jordan Pond
Otter Cliffs

sassy & spicy books

Storms of New England

Elusive Dreams   True Dreams
Stolen Dreams   Broken Dreams
Lost Dreams   Faded Dreams

Love on the Line

Wild Card Undercover   Running Target
Fatal Evidence   Hidden Betrayal
Death Race   Tactical Revenge

Acknowledgments

Thank you to so many people who have helped me along with my writing career. The most important, my husband and kids, who support me every step of the way. Em, who makes my words shine bright. Kris and Meredith, who are always there to help with the extra stuff. Emily, for sharing her Virginia knowledge of churches and potluck dinners. Kayla, for taking the time to chat with me about life in a small southern town. All the authors who give me encouragement and support and keep me sane, kind of. And to the people of fictional Prescott Hill, who came alive and welcomed me into their little town.

To my sister, Lynn, who dragged me to see that new science fiction movie, Star Wars, way back when. It was the start of a love affair for all things STAR related!

Chapter One

"*T*abby Cat, do you know where the plans are for the new addition?"

Tabitha Dailey looked up from her computer and forced a smile toward her father, Reverend Alfred Dailey, minister for the congregation at The Chapel on the Hill. The nickname grated. She was a grown woman of twenty-eight, not a child, and they were at work. She never called him "Daddy" when speaking to him in front of parishioners. Couldn't he keep the cutesy pet names out of the office?

"Of course I know where they are," she muttered to herself, then spoke louder. "They're right here, ready for the contractor. You made your decision, right?"

Her father scowled. "I said I'd have one chosen by today. Have you ever known me not to follow through on a project?"

"Never." She threw him the smile that always made him happy. Would he ever realize she wasn't?

"I had hoped to break ground by the middle of March, and we've only got a few weeks until then. I understand it'll be a bit to get permits and such. You've got the contracts ready to be signed, correct?"

"Right here, also." She tapped the credenza behind her with everything they'd need when meeting with the new contractor. Hopefully, it wasn't old man Bader and his son. They both drank too much. Unfortunately, her father had the credo that every man could be redeemed, and he should help those in need. What they didn't need was a crooked addition that would fall apart with a stiff wind.

She'd skimmed through each of the proposals when they came in and knew immediately that some wouldn't make the cut. If they weren't one of the congregation here at the Chapel in tiny little Prescott Hill, Virginia, they were plum out of luck. Not that her father would ever let anyone know it was one of his requirements.

"Who did you decide on?" The candidates were limited due to the congregation requirement, but her father had still wanted to go through everything and check out references. Like he couldn't have given them all a reference himself, but she supposed the way they constructed a building addition might be very different from how they conducted themselves in church. For their sake, she hoped it was true. The few who'd qualified wouldn't have been any choice of hers.

Intent on the book in his hands, he hadn't heard her. Nothing new. She loved her father. He was a wonderful man, but too often she wished he'd pay as much attention to her as he paid to his lost sheep. Maybe she needed to get lost more often.

A giggle made its way up through her throat, and she caught it before it escaped. Wouldn't the people of this town get a kick out of sweet, little Tabitha Daily, preacher's daughter, getting into trouble? Her best friends, Magnolia, Aubrey, and Kayla wouldn't be surprised. They knew how much she wanted to blow this popsicle stand of a town. Everyone else thought she would stay beside her dad as church secretary forever. Not if she could help it.

As her dad ambled closer, she clicked on the open tab and exited the theater's schedule. No sense him asking what movie she was checking times for. If she even suggested she might want to see a superhero or science fiction show, he'd get on his high horse about how ungodly they are and how she'd be better off spending her time in Bible study. Or at least watching some old movie from the forties when people had morals and scruples.

"I called the new man. He's going to meet us here shortly to sign the contracts and get the updated plans. I like the suggestions he's made for the addition, and he's very well thought of in this community. I know he'll do an excellent job."

"He? It's just one person, not a company?"

Finally looking at her, he nodded. "Yes, last minute bid. Only got it a few days ago. He came in far under what everyone else had quoted. I like that. Like that he didn't want to gouge us in God's house and get rich on the congregation's money."

Gouge us? She'd seen the bids, and most of them were fairly reasonable, especially the people from this community. Who had underbid all of them? Someone who already had money and didn't need it? The Prescotts and the Sinclairs were two of the wealthiest families in town, though neither of them owned a construction company. Most of the ones in the area barely got by, and the one who'd been building the new homes by the highway hadn't put in a bid. Why would they when they'd be making millions once those homes sold to new wealthy families who'd been flocking to the region lately?

Her father liked to think it was because of the church, his sermons, and the potluck dinner they had every Sunday after service. The gathering was famous for miles around, and many people came to socialize and enjoy the food. It was one of the reasons they needed an addition. She thought more people were getting away from the cities, since so many could work remotely now. Prescott Hill had an excellent internet provider, and setting up shop in your home was easier than ever. These city folks could now enjoy the beautiful rolling hills and farms of western Virginia while still earning their big city paychecks. Donovan Sinclair, her friend Maggie's fiancé, had done just that so he could be with her.

A sigh drifted out as she thought of how happy Maggie was. Would she ever find a love like that? Where a guy would give up almost everything for the woman of his dreams? Not with any of the men in this town. Even if they wanted her, she didn't want them. She had plans, and they didn't include being a church secretary for the rest of her life. Now to find a way to support herself when she moved away.

"Oh, here he is now." Her father gazed out the window into the parking lot, then moved to the door to greet their new contractor. "Of course, you know him. He comes to church every Sunday."

Tabitha rounded her desk. The man who'd entered was thin enough to hide behind her father's sturdy figure. They shook hands, then their new contractor stepped past and smiled.

Tabitha's heart dropped when she saw the shaggy brown hair and lean muscles on the tall figure. How in the world would she ever get through this addition with Wesley Roberts doing the work?

Wesley Roberts tipped his head at Tabitha and smiled. Too bad her own smile was forced. He knew the difference, had seen her fake one far too often. Why didn't she like him? Most people did.

"Hi, Tabitha. It's nice to see you again. You look pretty today."

Understatement. She was gorgeous with her long red hair that floated down her back with just a hint of wave. Adorable freckles that danced across her nose. Those lips that looked like they'd been kissed by strawberries. The fact she got him spouting poetry, even just in his mind, hadn't gone unnoticed. It happened far too often when he was in her presence.

The object of his affection glanced skeptically down at her simple blue dress, and her mouth pressed into a flat line. "Yeah, thanks. Are you the contractor for the addition?"

At his nod, her eyes narrowed. "Aren't you still working for Maggie? She didn't say anything about you leaving."

"I'm living in the bunkhouse until I get my own place finished up, and I help out when I can. However, I've been training Talia to do all the building repairs, and with the other kids there, I'm not needed as much. I figured I'd start to branch out and get other building jobs around town."

The truth was he'd never planned to stay at Magnolia's for the long haul. He'd stepped in when her father had passed because he knew she needed guidance on what to do with the farm and he'd been at a crossroads. Helping her get her buildings in better shape and working on the farm while living in the bunkhouse had allowed him the time to figure out his next step in life. Sad that at thirty-two he was finally getting his act together.

"You're working on your own place? What? You don't like living with a bunch of smelly guys who have been toiling over the land for endless hours?"

He loved her dry sense of humor. "It's the highlight of my day, but there comes a time when a man's got to make it on his own." Truer words were never spoken.

"Where's your new place? One of those fancy condos near the highway?" The lift of her lip showed what she thought of that.

Before he could answer, Reverend Dailey cleared his throat. "The contract, Tabitha. That's what Mr. Roberts has come here for, not chitchat. Save that for the Sunday potluck."

Wes wished he could chitchat with Tabitha more than just at the potluck. Most of the time, she ignored him. Ever since he'd met her a few years ago, he'd tried to catch her attention. Nothing seemed to work. What did he have to do to get her to view him as more than just another parishioner?

Besides being pretty, she was kind, funny, and intelligent. All traits he admired in a woman. She was also humble, which wasn't something he'd come across in his previous life in Roanoke. Her soft country beauty was a breath of fresh air when compared to the overly made up and perfumed ladies he'd escorted to events whenever his grandfather had beckoned. The more he saw her, the stronger his feelings grew.

This quaint little town of Prescott Hill was exactly what he needed to restart his life. If only Tabitha would give him a chance. She did something to him whenever she was around, but she'd blocked every attempt he'd made to ask her out.

Working on the church addition hadn't been in his plans, but with Maggie Popham hiring all the kids and not needing him as much, he'd found himself with extra time. With any luck, being near Tabitha every day would allow her to see him in a different light, and they could get to know each other better.

Reverend Dailey waved his hand toward the small conference room next to the church office. "We can go in here to discuss the project, and I can answer any questions you have."

As Wes followed the man inside, he peeked at Tabitha. Reverend Dailey saw his pause and nodded. "Tabitha, why don't you get a cup of coffee for Mr. Roberts? How do you take it?"

Wes waved her off. "I'm good. Thanks. Will Tabitha be involved with the project? Should she be in here with us? I understand she's essential to running the church."

He'd heard Maggie say that at one of the potlucks, though it hadn't sounded like it was a good thing when she'd said it. Tabitha's expression had dimmed, and he'd seen pain cross her face.

"Of course she is. I couldn't run this place without her."

The preacher's words didn't get the response he'd been hoping for. Tabitha's mouth tightened, and her eyes hardened.

"I suppose it wouldn't be a bad idea for us to take some notes in case you have any questions. Tabitha, can you grab a notepad and jot down any information we'll need?"

"Absolutely. I'll be right in."

In the room, Reverend Daily took the seat at the head of the table, so Wes sat to his right. When Tabitha arrived a moment later, he rose and started to pull out the chair next to him, but she crossed the room to sit on the other side of the table. Not unexpected with the way she'd avoided him in the past.

"Shall we begin?" The reverend slid the contract across the table until it sat in front of Wes, then retrieved another copy for himself.

They spent the next hour going over the specs, him asking questions and the minister hemming and hawing about what he wanted and when he wanted it by. Not all of his goals were attainable.

Finally, the pastor said, "I'm not all that good with details like hardware and curtains. I'm far too busy with my congregation to be bothered with the fripperies. Tabitha is the one you'll need to discuss those little things with. I hope you don't mind."

Wes felt like doing a cartwheel, but the redhead's stern expression brought him back to earth. "It'll be my pleasure. Thank you for trusting me with this project, Reverend Dailey. I won't let you or the congregation down."

"Good, good. Now, Tabitha, make sure he signs that contract, then give him a copy and make a few for our files. We'll have the first check ready to hand to you once I get the list of building supplies you'll be needing."

Wes stood and shook the minister's hand. "It shouldn't take me more than a few days to get a list and pricing for the initial supplies."

"Excellent. All that will go to Tabitha. I'll see you later. I've got a meeting soon."

Once the reverend was gone, Tabitha gathered her notepad and pencil. "Did you need any of this information typed up?"

He scribbled his name on the contract and picked it up. "I can just take that paper if it's easier. I don't want to make any more work for you."

"I'm not sure you'd be able to read my chicken scratch. It's a cross between shorthand and my failed cursive. But I can read it."

"Don't rush to get it done on my account. Whenever you have free time is fine. I've got quite a bit to do before I can even break ground. Permits, renting equipment, surveying."

"Great. Let me know if you need anything." Tabitha crossed the room, but Wes stepped in front of her.

"I'm sorry if what I said earlier upset you."

"What are you talking about?"

"When I suggested to your father that you were essential to running the church. You didn't seem to like it."

She shrugged and tried to pass.

He quickly handed her the contract. "Don't forget this. I'm looking forward to working with you, Tabitha."

Her lips pursed. "Listen, farm boy, we may have to work together to get this addition built, but don't go getting any ideas about us. You'll do your thing, and I'll do mine. Got it?"

He beat her to the door, then bowed low. "As you wish."

Chapter Two

*T*abitha's father marched out of his office with a smiling couple behind him. The expression on his face was one she knew well. These people were getting married. Today. Right now. Why couldn't anyone book things in advance?

"Can you find Daryl and bring him to the chapel? And put your nice dress on, please. As soon as I get the paperwork finished, these young people would like to become one in holy matrimony."

"Congratulations." Her smile was genuine, even though she was groaning inside. "I'll be right along." Once she found the handyman who cleaned the church, so they'd have a Best Man. She got to be the Maid of Honor. Again.

As she dug in the coat closet for one of the dresses she kept there for just such an occasion, she remembered Daryl had said he had a doctor's appointment today. Rats. They had to have another witness to the ceremony.

Whistling outside the window caught her attention, and she glanced up. Wes. Well, he'd said he'd be here today to start marking where the new addition would be. Guess he'd have to take a short break.

She tapped on the window and motioned for him to come inside. His head cocked to the side in confusion, so she smiled wider and waved him in. Yeah, inviting him closer wasn't typical of her.

When he peeked in her office, he said, "You wanted to see me?"

"Yes. Come on. It's time for a wedding." She picked up her dress and headed toward the ladies' room.

His eyes perked up. "You want to marry me? Kind of sudden, isn't it? You haven't even said yes to any of my requests for a date. My charm finally got to you, huh?"

Her frown punctured his bubble. "We have a couple in love who apparently can't wait to get married. You get to be a witness. Take that brown suit coat in the closet and put it on. I'll be out in a second."

The dress she had was easy on and easy off specifically for this reason, so she was back in her office in no time. The requisite silk flowers were pulled out of drawer, and she waved again for Wes to follow. The suit coat had been her father's and was more than a little baggy on his thinner frame. He pushed his sandy blond hair to the side as he stared at her. It honestly wasn't that long, just not the traditional men's cut her father expected of grown males. She kind of liked it, had wondered what it would feel like if she ran her fingers through it.

Stop. He is off limits. He wants to stay in town.

"You'll do. This shouldn't take more than fifteen minutes, unless my father gets long winded in his speech. Let's hope he doesn't."

One eyebrow rose on his face. "You do this often?"

"More than I'd like. You know the saying, 'Always a bridesmaid, never a bride'? That's me. The quintessential bridesmaid."

"If you really want to be a bride ..." He slipped his hand into hers and grinned.

"Don't even think that way, farm boy. I'm not ready for that yet."

She stalked off but caught his muttered, "As you wish." If it weren't for the fact she loved *The Princess Bride*, she would have been annoyed. After all, she did call him 'farm boy,' and he'd never once complained.

"Ah, there you are. Where's Daryl?" Her father glanced around the chapel.

"He had an appointment today. Wesley was happy to fill in."

"Joyously happy to," he echoed, and she gritted her teeth as she moved into place at the altar. After she handed the bride her bouquet, her father positioned Wes, then took his spot in front of the loving couple.

As the minister began the wedding spiel, Tabitha peeked over at Wesley. His boyish grin stayed firmly on his handsome face, the one she tried to ignore every time he came near. She routinely had to work up an attitude and reason for ignoring him, because, in all honesty, he was a great guy.

He wants to stay in Prescott Hill for the rest of his life. That was enough to avoid him and his charm. She already felt like she was drowning. Staying here forever would kill her for sure.

When her father got into his lecture about fidelity and focused his gaze on the happy couple, Tabitha sighed. They were fortunate they'd be moving out of town soon with the groom's new job, the reason for the quickie wedding. Her plan to leave this hick town was still in its infancy. When would she ever be able to save enough to get a place somewhere else?

The ceremony wound down, and soon the bride and groom were declared legally wed. Then, the marriage certificate was signed by all involved, and the newlyweds skipped off to start their new life of wedded bliss. Or so she hoped. As much as she hated being in these quickie weddings, she truly wished the couples had a long and joyous life together.

"Thank you for stepping in today, Mr. Roberts." Her father shucked his robe and strode toward his office still talking. "How's the addition coming along?"

They both hustled behind, Tabitha chuckling at the confused expression on Wesley's face. "Um, happy to help. I haven't actually done more than mark out where we'll put the foundation as I'm still waiting on the permits."

"If you don't get those soon, let me know. I'll put a bug in someone's ear at town hall to get them moving. Can't waste time."

And with that, they were dismissed. Tabitha took Wesley's arm and tugged him back toward her office where she held out her hand. "The coat?"

"Oh." He shrugged out of the jacket and handed it to her. "Are you going to change back into your other outfit?"

Glancing down at the pastel dress she wore, she sighed. It wasn't the fanciest dress in the world, but it was far prettier than anything else she was allowed to wear. Ridiculous at her age to still be letting her father dictate her wardrobe, but since she lived with him, it was often easier to wear something he'd approve of than listen to his disparaging comments. She'd learned to layer, then remove the outer layer once she left the house. Not that the final layer was in any way risqué.

"As it's only eleven, I suppose I should. Are you done for the day?"

"Not quite. I wanted to ask the reverend a few questions, but maybe you can help me."

"If I can." She knew every detail about this project, so it was unlikely they'd need to disturb her father. Only two days until Sunday, he'd be knee deep in revising his sermon and referencing the appropriate scriptures to go along with it.

Wes pointed his thumb over his shoulder. "Um, I need to show you a few things outside."

"Sure. Let me change first. No sense people driving past and seeing me prance around in the dirt with my bridesmaid dress on."

It took her only a few minutes to get back into her prim skirt and blouse and join Wes on the grass outside. He held the blueprints in his hands.

"Thanks. I just wanted to make sure I was lining this up the way your father wants it. This wall here," he pointed to the paper, "will be set against this wall, which will eventually be ripped down once the entire addition is airtight."

"Correct. He was hoping you could get this done during the warmer summer months."

"I'm a one-man show, but I'm pretty sure I can get the outer wall all sorted by then. All the little inside details may take longer, depending on exactly what he wants done. He's been rather vague."

Tabitha tried not to roll her eyes. Her father hated when she did that. Very disrespectful. "I'm not sure he knows what he wants. More room for the congregation is the primary goal. I sat with him and the architect to discuss where best to put the addition without ruining the quaint look of the building."

"Here in the back is the obvious place, though the pulpit and sanctuary will have to be moved into the new section, then add more rows of pews in the front."

"Maybe I can keep my regular seat and not be in the front row anymore." Her muttered comment had Wes grinning.

"If that was the case, the Sinclairs and Prescotts would be demoted to the middle of the chapel. Do you think Big Mama would allow that?"

Tabitha laughed. Mrs. Arabella Prescott, descendant of the town forefathers, would throw a fit if she wasn't in the first row. Doubtful Bitsy Beaumont-Sinclair would be happy either.

"I'm sure they'll demand front seats once the new section is added. The question will be if they'll want their pews with the gold nameplates to be moved to the front, or if they'd want some fancy new pews to sit in."

Wesley's eyes gleamed. "Fancy pews. Now let's imagine what they'd want in those fancy new pews."

"Big Mama would want a snack tray, so she can nibble on tidbits while my father rains fire and brimstone down upon us." The woman wasn't called Big Mama for nothing.

"Mrs. Beaumont-Sinclair would probably appreciate air conditioning or at the very least a fan blowing on her."

Tabitha laughed. "And extra padding on the cushions so she doesn't bruise her skinny behind."

"Maybe a rear-view mirror so she can see what the rest of the congregation is doing during the sermon." Wes mimicked craning his neck to look behind him.

"Especially now that her son, Donovan, has taken to sitting with the riffraff farmhands in the back."

Wes crossed his arms and puffed up his chest. "Who you calling riffraff?"

"I meant it in the kindest of ways. My best friend is part of that riffraff."

"Well, then, I won't take offense. Thanks for taking the time to make sure I've got these plans correct. I don't want to have the gates of Heaven shut as I get there because I messed up Reverend Dailey's new addition." He rolled up the plans and stuffed them into the tube.

"You'll be fine. Any questions, just ask. I probably know more about this addition than my father does. Not that he'd ever admit it."

"I kind of figured that." Wes winked.

Tabitha pivoted on her low sensible heels, then glanced back over her shoulder. "Thanks for helping out at the wedding today. Appreciate it."

As she crossed the grass, Wes shouted, "Not a problem. The next wedding is ours."

Chapter Three

*W*esley stood back and studied the progress of the new chapel addition. After he'd painstakingly dug the trenches and installed the frames for the footings, he'd hired a company to pour the concrete. The inspections had gone through fine, and he'd gotten help from some of the city kids Magnolia Popham had hired last year to help on her farm for the next steps. When she and Donovan had said they were hiring five kids who had aged out of the foster system to come to the country to live and work, he hadn't been too sure they'd work out. Thankfully, he'd been wrong. Of course, being treated like family by Maggie and Donovan had helped make the path easier.

Talia already knew how to do construction work, having been trained by one of her foster parents. Cary and Franklin had simply been there as brute strength. It had come in handy when they'd needed to build the frames, then maneuver them into place.

Today, he was on his own as some of the crops needed tending to. He'd take his time making sure there was space for the electrical and plumbing. The lumber for the frames should be arriving soon. He should probably let Reverend Daily know, so he could cut another check for the materials.

Not that Wes needed the money. He had plenty. More than he could spend in his lifetime. Some people could, but not him. He liked the simple life and couldn't imagine going back to the high life in the city.

The best thing was no one in Prescott Hill knew of his wealth. Or who his maternal grandfather was, thank God. The man had been ruthless in the banking business, giving out loans at bloated interest rates, calling in loans for missing one payment. He'd gotten rich on other people's misfortune. He hadn't cared one wit about the circumstances. Wes rarely spoke to him if he could at all avoid it. Thankfully, the money Wes had was from a trust fund his grandmother had left for him, money from her wealthy parents who had invested heavily in the railroad years ago. It had been a smart move and had secured a comfortable lifestyle for their kids and grandkids for years to come.

Since the townsfolk didn't know about his money, he had a pretty clear idea of who liked him for who he was. Back in Roanoke, he could never tell friend from gold digger. Would Tabitha see him in a different light if she knew his net worth?

Thinking about her must have conjured her up. She rounded the corner of the building, her father a step behind. He'd considered asking the reverend if he would be permitted to court his daughter. It was an old-fashioned notion, but her father seemed very much like an old-fashioned kind of person.

Then again, Tabitha might be a bit miffed if he did. He got the impression she was under her father's thumb far too much. The last thing he wanted to do was give her another reason to dislike him, though he was clueless as to what any of the other reasons were. All he knew was that she tried to avoid him if she could.

With the addition and her being the point man for information, they'd been thrust together these past three weeks. He'd tried his best to be polite and charming. Occasionally, he brought her coffee and muffins in the morning. She responded with a smile and a nod, then got back to work. If there was something else he could do, he didn't know what it was.

The reverend's eyes took in the construction, and Wes wondered what was on his mind. He'd know soon enough as the minister never minced words.

"Mr. Roberts. Good to see the progress you're making."

"Thank you, sir. It's coming along. I'll be getting the next shipment of supplies tomorrow."

Tabitha frowned and peered at her father. "I would think you'd need another check to cover that, won't you?'

Wes nodded slightly, but there was no reaction from the minister. Tabitha blew out a breath and tapped her father's arm. "Another check is needed for the new building material."

"What? Oh, of course. You can take care of that, Tabby Cat. I've got a meeting with the woman who runs the food pantry downtown. I'll see you this afternoon. Oh, and Mr. Roberts, nice job. Seems we're ahead of schedule. If you need to take some time off to go get a haircut, you've got my permission, though Tony's is open on Saturday mornings, too."

The man marched off. Tabitha remained, watching him leave. Once he was in the building, she peeked at Wesley.

"Don't get a haircut. He has no right to tell you to do anything that isn't associated with the new addition. You're a private contractor, and he has no control over your personal business."

Her narrowed eyes and tensed jaw on top of her arms crossed tightly over her chest made her seem like a rebel with a cause. Is this what her life had been like? Being controlled by her father on simple matters like a haircut? He hated to think it had.

"Does he have control over your personal stuff?" Wes kept his voice low and soft.

"He shouldn't." She kept her gaze at the building.

"But he does. Like what you wear?" He remembered how she'd eyed the pretty bridesmaid dress a few weeks back.

Tabitha glanced at the plain skirt and blouse she wore and scowled. "Dress code for the church office is professional attire."

"Does that include Sunday service, too?"

Her mouth thinned, and the light in her eyes dimmed. He hated seeing it.

"Not that you don't look lovely during the sermon. You do." He thought she'd look lovely wearing a paper sack.

She gave a tight little laugh. "Right? In my plain little dress and flat shoes, while everyone else is wearing the latest designer labels, killer heels, and a fancy hat."

It had struck him as strange how much the people of this town dressed up for church. It was like a competition to see who could outdo the other. Maybe that's why Tabitha had caught his eye. She wasn't playing games and trying to impress. Of course, now he wondered if that was only because her father wouldn't allow it.

"You wear a hat."

Her eyes rose in disgust. "Yes, the same one every week. Pristine white and plain. My father nearly had a cow when he saw it had a bow on the back of it. I had to convince him I got it cheap at a thrift shop. Heaven forbid anyone think the preacher's daughter is so vain she needs to spend the congregation's money on fancy clothes."

"You earn a salary from your job here, right? Why can't you spend it on whatever you want?"

"It wouldn't be frugal. My father is all about being frugal and not flaunting material possessions."

An idea came to him. "What if someone bought a fancy hat for you? Would he allow that?"

She finally peered his way. "Who's going to buy me a fancy hat? It would look ridiculous with all my drab conservative dresses, anyway."

Her shoulders drooped, and she sighed. Was this the time to tell her he was rich and could take her away from all this? Not if he wanted her to fall in love with Wes, the man, and not Wes, the trust fund kid.

"I'm sorry, Tabitha. Even with plain clothes and a simple hat, I still think your beauty shines through more than most of the congregation."

A smile bloomed on her gorgeous face. Her eyes were damp as she nodded at him. "Thank you. That's so sweet." Her expression quickly turned neutral. "But I'm still not going on a date with you."

He couldn't help the laugh that made its way out. She was consistent. He'd give her that. With a shrug, he said, "Not this week maybe. I'll keep trying."

Chapter Four

*G*lancing around the chapel, Tabitha frowned at the beautiful new outfits all the women wore. Why couldn't her father see she stood out like a dull sheep among the white fluffy ones? After her conversation with Wesley last week, she felt more conscientious than ever. She didn't fit in here.

Wasn't allowed to fit in here.

Maggie strolled past her with Donovan on her arm, waving as they did. Her friend always looked like a million bucks. Her clothes usually came from a thrift store, but the woman knew how to shop and find the designer labels. Now that she was marrying a Sinclair, she could afford to buy the name brands firsthand. Tabitha was thrilled for her friend but couldn't help the envy that crept up on her at times. She had to push it back. It wouldn't do for the preacher's daughter to be seen exuding one of the Seven Deadly Sins.

A few minutes later, Wes entered the chapel. Quickly, she brushed her hands over her drab skirt and straightened her hat. What was she doing? She didn't care what Wesley Roberts thought of her. Did she? No.

Another of the sins hit her. Pride. She shouldn't care what she looked like or how people saw her. But she did. It was bad enough everything she wore was plain with a high collar or neckline and neutral in color, but her father insisted she buy her wardrobe a size larger. He didn't want her wearing anything that was too snug or form fitting. Men might get the wrong idea about her.

What idea? That she was a woman? Ridiculous.

Her thoughts got pushed away as the choir began to sing and her father entered, then climbed into the pulpit to begin his sermon. Plenty of fire and brimstone today to put the fear of God into all these sinners, yet here sat his daughter, wishing she could be anywhere else.

When the choir stood for their final hymn, Tabitha breathed a sigh of relief. She still had work to do setting up the potluck, but soon she'd be free to gab with her friends and enjoy herself. Usually, her father didn't police her as much during the dinner. He was too busy schmoozing with those who might donate heavily to the new addition fund. He'd already put a bug in her ear about chatting it up with Donovan Sinclair and his parents. Like she wanted to have a donation conversation with Drake and Bitsy Sinclair. Not in this century.

Once the food had been laid out on the table and Big Mama had clapped her hands stating it was time to eat, the scurry began. Tabitha, being the dutiful daughter, had to wait until everyone else had gone through the line before she got her own food. Often, the really good stuff had already been finished off.

Finally, she strolled past the half empty casserole dishes, scooping out what looked good. Fortunately, most of the more well-off parishioners donated larger portions, so some of the less fortunate souls could have leftovers to take home. It was something she loved about this community—their willingness to help others. Too bad they couldn't help her find a way to get away from her boring life. What twenty-eight-year-old still lived with her father?

Glancing across the pavilion, she made her way over to where her friends sat. As usual, they'd saved a spot for her. Once she'd settled in between Kayla and Aubrey, across from Magnolia and Donovan, she said a quick prayer of thanks for the meal and dug in.

Aubrey tipped her over-sized sunglasses to the end of her nose, then pushed back a strand of her mulberry-colored hair. "How's it been working with Wes on the addition project?"

"He's outside doing the construction, and I'm inside doing my usual tedious job."

Kayla flipped one of her dark, corkscrew curls over her shoulder and smirked. "He doesn't get a break every now and then? You know, come inside for a drink of water and a little conversation?"

Tabitha stuffed her mouth with food to keep from having to respond. Of course, that was the moment Wesley chose to wander by with his heaping plate. Donovan and Maggie slid over, allowing him to squeeze in. Right across from her. Seriously? Couldn't her friends understand she didn't want to stare at the handsome man while she ate? Maybe if she got something stuck in her teeth and chewed really loud, he'd be turned off. It could work.

Conversation changed to the spring planting season and how the kids Maggie had brought from the city were working out. Because of them, Wes was able to do the church addition.

"How's the work on the church coming along, Wes? We miss you at the farm." Donovan nodded at his friend, then took a sip of his sweet tea.

"The construction is right on schedule. Thanks for allowing me to use a few of the kids last week. Granted, it would go faster if I didn't have to take time during the day for a wedding. I have to admit that Tabitha sure does look nice holding flowers while the preacher talks of love and marriage. Wasn't our wedding beautiful, Tabitha?"

She threw him the evil eye as her friends all stared, mouths open. "It wasn't *our* wedding. We were witnesses to a couple who apparently couldn't wait."

Wesley's eyes gleamed, his hand to his chest. "It was a beautiful thing and definitely gave me ideas. I can't wait until we have our own."

Tabitha growled and rose. "I'm going to get a piece of Mrs. Mancini's pie before it's all gone."

As she walked away, Maggie followed. "He was only kidding, you know. Don't be so hard on him."

At the table, she picked up a dessert plate and strolled to the end where the pies were Unfortunately, Mrs. Mancini's were all gone, as they always were. She went with Cissy Hanson's chocolate cream instead. "I know he's only kidding. I just wish I wasn't the butt of his jokes."

"He really likes you, Tab. Give the guy a chance. What's so wrong with him?"

After scooping an extra-large piece of pie, making sure her father didn't see her embracing the next deadly sin of gluttony, she faced her friend. "There's nothing wrong with him. That's the problem. He's adorably cute in a shaggy dog kind of way. He's a hard worker, a great friend, makes me laugh too often, and says some of the sweetest things I've ever heard." She shoved a forkful of the pie in her mouth, humming at the delicious flavor.

"And the problem is?"

"He wants to stay in this town. He's building his own house at the moment."

"You know I hate that you don't plan to stay here with us."

Careful of her pie, Tabitha gave Maggie a one-armed hug. "If I stay here, I'll always be under my father's thumb. Look at what you're wearing compared to me. I know you're going to say you got it secondhand, but regardless, my father would never allow me to wear something that pretty. And it's not just the clothes. It's everything. I'm too old to be taking orders from my parent. I need to break free." Another piece got eaten as she made sure her father didn't see her stuffing it in her mouth like a pig. She'd probably gain ten pounds. Why couldn't she be like Aubrey who chowed like a linebacker and never gained weight?

Magnolia sighed. "I understand. There's not much I can do to change your father, but I can help in the clothing department. Next week is Easter. What had you planned to wear?"

Tabitha rolled her eyes. "Probably that tan dress with the small pink flowers. It's better than most of my Sunday outfits. My white hat doesn't match it, though."

"I have an idea. Donovan took me to Roanoke and forced me to buy some fancy Sunday dresses."

"Forced you?" Tabitha laughed, scraping the filling off her plate.

"I had work to do on the farm, okay? Anyway, I got a dozen new dresses because he loves seeing me all dolled up and showing up his mother at the service."

Tabitha tried not to grin. "You are so lucky."

Maggie took a quick peek at her fiancé. "I am. I know. But with the new dresses, I need to get rid of some of my older ones to make room in the closet. Donovan says I don't have to shop at the thrift store any longer."

"You still will, though." Tabitha licked her fork clean.

Maggie laughed. "Probably. I spent too many years being frugal. I need to teach my future husband how to do it. But I need closet space."

Tabitha wished she had enough clothes to fill her closet. "You want to give me your old dresses? I'm not sure my father would allow some of the ones you've worn."

"Some of them, probably not. But you'd fit in that gorgeous, peach Ralph Lauren dress, and it will look awesome on you. It's flattering while still being conservative. It would be perfect for Easter. Tell your father I insist. I'll be a Sinclair soon, and he can't afford to be making a Sinclair upset."

The peach dress had always been one of Tabitha's favorites. She and Maggie were similar size, so it would definitely look nice on her. Her white hat would go with it, too. It was a tired piece she was loathe to wear on yet another Sunday, but she had few choices unless she wanted the wrath of the reverend upon her.

"Okay. Maybe. Bring it over, and we'll see if I can make it happen."

Chapter Five

*T*abitha dropped her purse on the shelf in the closet and headed to her desk. Draped over it was a hanger with a peach dress covered in plastic. A gorgeous wide-brimmed hat sat next to it.

Magnolia must have left the dress for her. But the hat? Her friend hadn't said anything about a hat, and Tabitha had never seen this one. Had she purchased one to match?

Picking up the hat, she examined it. The weave was beautiful, and there was a small cluster of flowers gathered on the side with tiny ribbons interwoven. It even had some small feathers tucked into the cluster. Oh, my. This was finer than anything she'd ever owned. It would be the perfect Easter bonnet for this Sunday. For once, she wouldn't be the frumpy lady in the front row.

She placed the hat on her head, tilted it at an angle, then peered into the reflection on her computer screen. A tiny sigh escaped from her mouth at how perfect it was. If Maggie had bought this, she wouldn't be able to accept it. Even though her friend was marrying a man who came from money, Donovan was still getting his new business in Prescott Hill up and running, and Maggie had a farm to run and hands to pay.

It looked amazing, though, and would be the ultimate accessory to the dress. She could pay Maggie back. Then, she wouldn't feel so guilty.

"Tabitha." Her father frowned from the doorway.

Quickly, she removed the hat and tossed it next to the dress.

"That's a little ostentatious, isn't it?"

His reaction was exactly what she'd expected and why she'd balked at accepting Maggie's help. But this hat was so beautiful. Greed. Another one of those deadly sins. It settled deep inside and strengthened her backbone.

"It's far less than most of the hats women will be wearing at Sunday service. Everyone will be going all out for Easter Sunday, wearing their newest and best outfits. I'll be surprised if Mrs. Prescott doesn't have a peacock on her head."

Her father's chuckle startled her, especially followed by a tiny grin. Then, he cleared his throat and grew solemn. "How much did that cost you? We can't be frivolous with the congregation's money."

"The congregation's money? What about the money I earn from doing this job? Why is it wrong of me to buy something I want with my money? No one tells Mr. Prescott at the bank not to buy his Cuban cigars with the money he earns from the bank. It's all other people's money originally." Had that been too much? She'd never spoken back to her father this way.

The frown on his face got deeper, then he sighed. "As much as I see your point and agree, we can't be flaunting wealth when so many of our residents have much less than we do. We need to set an example of frugality and simplicity."

"I understand, but this hat is a gift, and it matches the dress Maggie gave me to wear for Easter. I haven't had anything this nice in years."

"I suppose Magnolia doesn't need to be frugal anymore, what with marrying a Sinclair," her father said, his eyes softening.

"She still will be. That's just who Maggie is," Tabitha replied. "But every now and then she'll splurge and buy herself something special."

Cocking his head toward the dress and hat, her father's lips turned up slightly at the corners. "Well, enjoy her hand-me-downs. It is pretty, and I suppose you deserve something special yourself every now and then. Your mother always used to buy you a pretty Easter bonnet. I think she'd like this one." He about-faced and marched out of her office and into his own.

She quickly picked up the dress and hung it in the closet so it didn't wrinkle, then gently placed the hat on the credenza behind her. She couldn't stop staring at it and thinking she'd actually get to wear it with her dad's approval. Maybe she'd even wear her cream kitten heels instead of flats. It was Easter, after all.

Well ... the bulletin needed to be done today and printed, and she had to go over more of the design details with Wesley on the addition. She might as well get started.

Two hours later, she'd managed to check off almost everything in her planner. Now, she got to sit around and tidy things up and appear busy for another few hours. Maybe she should call Maggie and say thank you. It was lunch time, after all, and her friend would most likely be in the house.

The phone rang only twice before the call connected.

"Maggie, the dress is beautiful. Thank you so much."

"Oh, I'm happy to pass it on. Does it fit okay?"

"I haven't had a chance to try it on yet. Dad is still here, and you know how he is about taking time from the workday for anything personal."

Maggie gave a sad laugh. "I'm sure it will be a perfect fit. Can't wait to see you in it on Sunday."

"I can't wait either. And that hat is something else. It took some fancy talking to get Dad okay with it. Did you buy it specifically, because I don't remember you ever wearing it with the dress?"

"Uh, I didn't give you a hat. Only the dress."

Another glance behind her confirmed she hadn't imagined it. "The dress showed up on my desk with a gorgeous matching hat next to it. If it wasn't you, then who put it there?"

Maggie hummed. "I gave the dress to Wes yesterday to drop off today since I had tons of stuff to do on the farm. I never pictured him as the hat buying type, but maybe …"

The conversation she'd had with Wes a week ago ran through her mind. They'd talked about hats and her lack of choice when it came to buying clothes. Tears pricked the back of her eyes at the thought he'd done this for her.

"Thanks, Maggie. I'll figure this out. See you Sunday."

After ending the chat with her friend, she studied the hat once more. It appeared brand new but no tags were attached.

Whistling outside her office had her head whipping up. Wes hovered in the hallway, peering her way. She pointed to the hat, then at him, tilting her head in question.

He shrugged and nodded.

"Thank you," she mouthed, a smile blossoming on her face.

Anxiously, Wes gazed toward her father's office door, which luckily was closed, and grimaced.

Tabitha quickly gave him a thumbs up, causing his eyes to gleam and that adorable grin to appear. He had to stop being so nice to her. It was breaking down all her walls of resistance where he was concerned. She couldn't have that or her plans for her future would end up tossed out like yesterday's trash.

Chapter Six

"**H**appy Easter." Wesley waved and called out to the parishioners that he knew, which were most of them at this point. He'd been in this town for almost two years and had met many of the people in the community, in part due to the weekly potluck The Chapel had on Sunday.

Entering the church, he allowed his eyes to adjust to the surroundings. Tabitha sat in her usual spot at the end of the front row, looking like a ray of sunshine in her pretty dress and matching hat. The Prescotts took up most of the front right while Drake and Bitsy Sinclair occupied the left. With their only son, Donovan, escorting Magnolia and sitting in her usual pew in the back, there was room between them and Tabitha.

Normally, he'd give her a smile and a nod, then follow the rest of Maggie's farmhands to the back, but today the object of his affection practically glowed. He liked to think it was the hat he'd given her that had added to her confidence. Maybe it was just the fact it was Easter.

Whatever the reason, he didn't want to sit with the farmhands. He wanted to sit with her. As more of the congregation arrived and strolled past, her mouth turned down. Every week she sat by herself. Could be it was time to change that.

"May I sit with you?"

Tabitha glanced behind her. The church was more crowded than usual due to the holiday.

"Don't you typically sit with Maggie's crew?"

He shrugged. "Yeah, but I'm not working for the farm anymore. I'm working for the church, so I thought I should sit with the church crew."

"All one of me. Well, it's a free pew. Help yourself."

Once he got himself settled beside her, he had to exert a lot of control not to watch her every second. When he thumbed through the bulletin, he could see her dainty hands clenched together in her lap. Was she uncomfortable with him sitting here? God, he hoped not.

As the guys from the farm filtered in, they gave him sly looks and grins. He didn't care. He didn't work with them anymore, and being beside Tabitha was a dream come true. If she actually wanted him next to her, it would be even better.

The choir filed in, and everyone rose. He pressed his lips near her ear and whispered, "You're beautiful today." Aw, seriously? That implied only today. She was beautiful every day. Couldn't he get anything right?

A blush covered her cheeks. "It's the hat."

"I think it's the lady wearing the hat."

Before she could dispute his statement, the choir began their first hymn. He flipped the hymnal to the correct page and sang along. Tabitha's sweet voice rang out next to him. Why she wasn't in the choir, he didn't know. She had the voice of an angel.

Sitting next to her was excruciating and heaven all at the same time. He wasn't sure he heard a word the preacher said. His attention was focused on the pretty redhead practically glued to his side with the extra crowd in church today.

Every time their hands accidentally touched, something he made sure to do often, Tabitha sucked in a breath of air and stiffened. Was she as affected as he was by the contact? That would be good. Or did it turn her off so much she was appalled? Hopefully not. By the time the choir sang the final note of the last song, he was sweating. He hadn't wanted to do anything to make her upset with him.

When the preacher exited and the choir filed out, Tabitha adjusted her hat and headed for the door. Wesley bolted after her. "Can I help you with set up today?" Why he was asking, he didn't know. He helped every week and had never sought permission to do so.

"That would be nice. Thanks."

Tabitha held the door to outside while he and several others transported platters and bowls to the waiting tables under the pavilion. There was substantially less food in the downstairs refrigerator today. Being a holiday, many of the families would likely be having their main meal at home.

Magnolia and Donovan nipped over and gave quick hugs to Tabitha. Wes paused on his way back to the fridge.

"Have you had enough of us, Wes?" Maggie asked as she embraced him. "You aren't sitting with us in our pews anymore."

"I'm working at the church now."

"It looks like you're staying for the potluck today, so I assume you won't be having Easter dinner at the farm."

Maggie's expression had color rising in his cheeks. She knew why he was staying at the potluck today. It had nothing to do with being tired of the farm and everything to do with the pretty redhead standing next to him.

"You have so many mouths to feed you won't even miss me."

Donovan shook his hand. "I'll miss you. The bunkhouse isn't the same with only the two old coots and the young kids. It was nice having someone my age to even things up."

"It's only a few months before you get married, then you'll be up at the big house with Ms. Magnolia. Figured I'd better ease on out while I could."

"Thanks." A scowl on his face, Donovan gave Wes a good-natured slap on the back.

"Well, have a Happy Easter, both of you. My regards to all the hands."

Maggie squeezed Tabitha's hand. "We're still on for Wednesday night, right? Kayla's place?"

"I wouldn't miss it," she said. "I love these prayer meetings my dad's been going to each week."

Maggie chuckled. "Especially the fact they're a few towns over and leave you with at least three or four hours of free time."

Tabitha smirked. "Definite bonus. Not that I'd tell him that."

As the friends continued to talk, Wes got a better picture of how stifling Tabitha's life was. Could he find a way to help her out? Get a little more excitement into her life. Something that wouldn't irritate her father?

Maggie and Donovan waved as they took off, then their other friend, Kayla, said her goodbyes.

"I've got to get home to help Mom. My brothers always offer, but they spend more time sampling the food than preparing it. I'll see you Wednesday night."

Wes nipped inside to make sure all the food had been put out, then dashed back out. Big Mama clapped her hands and announced it was time to eat. The Prescotts took their role of town founders seriously. They'd enjoy the potluck now, then have their family Easter dinner at the supper hour.

Making his way down the table, he searched out a certain lady. As usual, she waited at the end of the line for all to go through. Today, there were far fewer, though the food could feed twice the amount here. It was one of the things he loved about this community. There might be a few snobs who peered down their noses at others, but everyone made sure to take care of those in need. Each week, those who could supplied a larger amount than their family could eat, thus allowing others to bring leftovers home. The food was packed up in containers and situated on the end of the tables. Somehow, it always got into the hands of those who needed it without a fuss or any attention brought to who took it.

Wes timed pouring his glass of sweet tea so that Tabitha was done filling her plate as he was ready to find a table. She beelined it to where her friend, Aubrey, sat. A few other townsfolk were nearby, but there was plenty of space for both Tabitha and him. He scooted in right next to her on the bench, ducking to avoid the brim of her hat.

Aubrey adjusted her huge sunglasses to the tip of her nose. "You look fab today, Tab. I know the dress is Maggie's, but that hat is out of this world. There's no way your father bought it for you. It doesn't seem like it came from a thrift store either. It's too new."

Tabitha threw him a swift glance before answering. "It was a gift from a friend, but my dad thinks it was a Maggie hand-me-down. I didn't bother correcting him, since I didn't actually pay for it."

"Good girl." Aubrey swiped at the purple bangs that fringed over her eyebrows. Her Easter hat was a small woven number that matched her dress. It also had a few feathers protruding from a bow in the side. Between these two and what the rest of the congregation wore on their heads, most of the birds in the area must be flying around naked.

"Who'd you inherit your purple hair from? Mom or Dad?" he jokingly asked Aubrey. The rest of her colorful hair hung out and scooped up near her neck.

Pursing her lips, Aubrey shook her head. "Neither, and it's mulberry. Do you have a problem with my hair?" Her tone indicated others had.

"No. I kind of like it. Blonde and brunette are so overrated."

Aubrey peered over her sunglasses again. "Not redheads?"

The grin popped out before he could stop it. "I confess to having an affinity for red hair. Freckles, too. It's my weakness."

He caught Tabitha's eye roll. "Why aren't you having Easter dinner at the farm?"

"I don't live there any longer."

Her head whipped up, eyebrows together. "I knew you were building a house. I didn't realize you'd already finished it. Maggie didn't tell us."

Aubrey pushed her green bean casserole around on her plate with her fork. "I suppose Mags is kind of busy with her wedding plans and dealing with her future mother-in-law."

The two women both winced. He had to agree. Bitsy Beaumont-Sinclair wasn't someone he'd want to go up against. He'd heard enough from Donovan to want to stay clear of the woman.

After taking another bite, Aubrey asked, "Where's your new place?"

"It's near the Old Johnson Farm. I've got a little over ten acres along the New River."

Tabitha tipped her head. "Are you getting rid of the big ring of rocks all the teenagers used for partying?"

He'd seen the location and had heard from some locals about the events. "Did you frequent the place, Ms. Dailey? I can't imagine the reverend approving of that nighttime activity."

"Oh, he didn't." Aubrey tapped the table in front of Tabitha's plate. "We used to sneak her out after he went to bed. Had to make sure to get her back quietly. He never suspected a thing."

Wes chuckled and splayed his hand dramatically on his chest. "I would never have expected it of you. You surprise me, Tabitha. In a good way."

What she was thinking as she gazed at him, he didn't know. He wished he did. Wished her thoughts were warm and accepting.

"I never drank more than a glass or two of wine. Tame compared to some of the kids there. Now, what about the rocks? You never answered."

"The ring is right on the edge of my property, but I've built the house on the other side. I doubt I'd be able to see or hear if anyone goes down there."

Aubrey grinned. "I'll have to pass the news on to the local teenagers. What kind of house have you built? Something better than the bunkhouse, I assume."

He shrugged. "I think so. It's nothing pretentious. Just a log cabin. I don't need anything super fancy, especially after living in the bunkhouse for a few years."

A sigh escaped from Tabitha's perfect lips. "I imagine just being by yourself is heaven. Not having to deal with the other farmhands or any unwanted neighbors."

"It's definitely quiet, and I like the privacy."

Her expression of longing grew as she stared into the distance. "That would be incredible."

If she'd lived with her father her entire life, she'd probably never had any kind of privacy. Was there something he could do to help her? And would she actually let him?

Chapter Seven

Kayla opened the door and welcomed her friends. Tabitha shuffled in with the pizzas while Aubrey followed her with bags of chips and dip.

"Where's Maggie?" Kayla peered around them into the empty hallway.

"Probably smooching up that handsome fiancé of hers." Aubrey pursed her mulberry-stained lips. "I'll bet it's hard to peel herself away."

Footsteps pounded up the stairs, and Maggie popped into view. "I heard that. I can control myself when it comes to Donovan."

Kayla raised an eyebrow. "So you aren't late because you were kissing him a few more times?"

Glancing at her watch, Maggie frowned. "I'm not late. Though maybe I did give him a few more kisses than usual. No one was around. I have to take advantage when I can."

As they entered Kayla's apartment and deposited their goods on the kitchen table, Tabitha sighed. "We're all just envious that you found such a great guy who loves you so much."

Maggie, Kayla, and Aubrey froze in place and stared at her.

"What?"

Aubrey planted her hands on her hips. "Pretty sure Wesley Roberts has a massive case of love and affection he's been tossing in your direction, Miss Dailey. You aren't taking advantage."

Kayla held her hand up. "Don't say he isn't a great guy. We all know he is."

Tabitha scooped up a paper plate, slid a piece of pizza on it, then hustled out to Kayla's balcony overlooking the New River. Her friends followed. She didn't want to discuss Wesley Roberts. However, she doubted they'd give up on the subject.

Once ensconced in their chairs, Maggie picked up where they'd left off. "Wes is crazy about you, Tab. You've got to know that."

After chewing and swallowing a cheesy bite, she tipped her head. "He's got a crush on me, sure. I wouldn't call it love. Don't forget he has this burning desire to stay in Prescott Hill for the rest of his life."

"We're here," Aubrey reminded her, igniting a twinge of guilt that always arose when she talked of leaving town. "You should want to stay with us."

Kayla nodded. "You two looked awfully cute and cozy sitting together in church on Easter."

"You do make a handsome couple," Maggie added.

Tabitha glared at her friends. She loved them, but they didn't fully understand her need to be free of her father's rules.

"*He* sat with me. I didn't really have a choice, unless I wanted to make a scene. Hardly appropriate for the preacher's daughter to tell someone to go bug off while in the Lord's house."

"I wish we could make your dad understand your needs and wants." Aubrey played with her bangs, brushing them out of her eyes. She didn't have any family around, and Tabitha felt bad any time she complained about her father. At least he was here and loved her.

"Living with him wouldn't be so bad if he didn't police everything I read and watch. I'm a grown woman. I can make my own decisions."

"It's ridiculous that he still does this." Kayla chomped on some chips. "It was bad enough when you were a kid."

Tabitha snorted. "He never even let me read or watch anything Harry Potter. I only saw Star Wars because you and your brothers were watching that marathon at your house, Kayla. If I didn't have the library to go to or the sleepovers at all your houses, I never would have known how amazing science fiction and fantasy is."

"Didn't you need to hide the books you brought home from the library?" Aubrey asked, finishing off her third piece of pizza. How did she stay so thin?

"I never brought any home unless they were children's Bible stories. He would have freaked. Going to the library was an acceptable activity, and I wasn't about to risk getting it taken away. If he ever checked in with Mrs. Goodwin, the librarian, all she could tell him was that I was in one of the comfy chairs on the second floor, reading. Luckily, he never found out what I was reading."

"There was nothing wrong with what you were reading," Kayla huffed. "It's fiction. Made up. Isn't real. Fun to read."

All their lives, her friends had been as frustrated as Tabitha with what she hadn't been allowed to do. They'd taken turns having her sleep over and go on outings with their own families so she could live a little. It had gotten worse after her mom had died.

Tabitha tossed her empty plate on the low table. "Those two half-finished books I wrote that I printed out at your place, Maggie, they're hidden under my bed still. I didn't dare leave them on my computer in case he found them."

Maggie blinked. "You don't have them in some sort of file?"

Pulling her keys from her pocket, Tabitha palmed the flash drive attached. "I've got them in here. It looks like a fancy key chain. He doesn't realize what's in it."

Aubrey closed one eye. "Please, tell me you have those short stories you write for the science fiction magazine on there. How many have you written?"

Tabitha had told her friends that she dabbled in writing science fiction stories and had e-mailed a few to them. Since none of them were as big a fan as she was, she hadn't shared all that much. They supported her a hundred percent, but she knew the interest wasn't there, and that was okay with her. She'd never want anyone to read her work just for the sake of reading. Tabitha grinned, thinking of the one big secret she'd kept from her father. "I'm at thirty-five chapters now. Of course, they're only a few thousand words a pop. Since they've gotten such a great response, though, the magazine keeps asking me for more. The next one comes out in the July edition."

"And they're all related?" Aubrey guzzled the rest of her sweet tea like she'd been in the desert.

"Each story can be read by itself, but if you put them all together, it shows a very complex world where many of their lives interconnect. I'd love to flesh out each chapter and combine them into a novel."

Maggie tilted her head. "Your father doesn't know about any of it? Aren't you afraid some parishioner will see your name on the stories and tell him?"

Heat seeped into Tabitha's face, and she bit her lip. "I use a pen name."

"What?" All three of them scooted closer, and Aubrey said, "You never told us you have a pen name."

"I figured, if you didn't know, you couldn't tell anyone. Not that I think you'd snitch on me, but sometimes things pop out when you don't want them to."

Kayla stuck her little finger out. "If we pinky swear never to breathe a word of your pen name to anyone, will you tell us what it is?"

Maggie and Aubrey had their pinkies out and connected in a flash. Tabitha took a deep breath and joined her finger to theirs. "This is science fiction, so it's kind of weird. Plus, I don't want anyone knowing I'm a woman, so I went for something that could be either."

Aubrey tugged on their hands. "Give, girl!

Taking a deep breath, she said, "It's Tempus Elgato." What would they think? That she was crazy?

Maggie smirked. "Cool. Still kind of you without being you."

"You figured it out already." Tabitha wrinkled her nose. She thought she'd been clever.

"What are you talking about?" Kayla asked.

"Tempus means time in Latin." Maggie held up one finger. "Her last name is Dailey. It's a measure of time."

"Oh, wait!" Aubrey jumped up and down. "El gato means cat in Spanish. Your dad calls you Tabby Cat. Ha!"

"You are brilliant, Tabitha." Maggie squeezed her hand. "You're also twenty-eight years old. I think you should be able to read, write, and watch whatever you want."

She couldn't disagree, but she was the one who had to live with her father if she did something he didn't approve of. Regardless of how adorable Wes was and how much he seemed to like her, she couldn't fall for him and be stuck in Prescott Hill her entire life. The thought of that filled her with despair.

Chapter Eight

Wesley picked up his insulated bag and wandered over to the pavilion where Tabitha just happened to be eating her lunch. Often, she ate at her desk, but with the excellent weather today and her father speaking at a luncheon for the ladies of the Three Oaks Country Club, she must be feeling daring.

"Oh, hey. Didn't realize you were out here, too." *Liar.* He'd burn in hell for sure with all the fibbing he did to get closer to Tabitha.

She lifted her hand and indicated the seat across from her. As she took in the cloudless sky and slight breeze, her shoulders lifted and fell.

"Perfect day to be outside," he commented as he plunked onto the bench.

She actually smiled at him. "It is. I'm tempted to skip out of work and play hooky. It's too nice to be inside today."

Once he'd taken a small bite of his sandwich, he asked, "How much do you still need to do?"

"Nothing really. My father doesn't realize he could get by with a part-time secretary. He hires out for so many of the tasks that it doesn't leave much for me to do."

"Have you mentioned this to him?"

She took a sip of her sweet tea and nodded. "Yes, but he likes having me under his thumb. Thinks giving me a full-time job is what's expected of a father. I'd rather be anywhere but here."

"What would you rather be doing?"

"Something creative." She stared at her sandwich before taking a bite.

"Like your friend, Aubrey? Doesn't she repaint old furniture and sell it?"

She gave a half smile. "That's part of what she does. It's a bit more than just painting furniture. I'm not much into art, but there are other ways to be creative."

"True, like building a church addition. To a point. The architect who drew the plans is probably more creative than me."

"But you still get to build with your hands. Create something. I'm at a desk typing up e-mails and recording donations."

"There's nothing wrong with that."

"It is if you hate what you do. I'm bored. I need some excitement in my life. I'm slowly dying here in this town."

Reaching across the table, he patted her hand. "I don't think it's the town that's killing you. You just need something to help spice up your life."

The smirk on her face made her look adorable. "I suppose you're just the person to spice things up for me."

"I can hardly blast off in a spaceship and take you to other planets, but maybe I can liven things up a bit."

"I'd love to blast off to another planet." Her gaze roamed the sky longingly.

"How would you want to get there?"

"What do you mean, how?"

"The Starship Enterprise. Millennium Falcon. Moya. Serenity. Stargate. TARDIS. Lots of ways to travel."

She pursed her lips. "Well, I wouldn't really be blasting off if I went through the Stargate. More like walking through."

She hadn't even blinked at some of his suggestions. "You know what all of those are?"

Her cheeks grew rosy, and she lowered her eyes. "Don't let my father know. He thinks science fiction can warp the soul."

Wes sighed, realizing how tough her life had been. "He knows it's fiction, pretend, right? Stuff people created because they were probably bored? Maybe typing up e-mails."

Tabitha laughed, and her shoulders lowered. "He thinks everyone should read only the Bible and spiritual books."

"Understandable for a man in his position, but not everyone likes to read the same thing."

"You try and make him see that. He still thinks I'm a little girl who needs to be taken care of."

Wes would love to take care of Tabitha, but he doubted she'd appreciate knowing that. "So, how are you traveling to the stars? You never answered."

Her eyes twinkled. "Out of the ones you mentioned, hmm ... maybe Moya. It would be cool being on a living ship."

"As long as you don't have Peacekeepers trailing after you, right?"

"Right. A Leviathan would be a very neat place to live, especially since they'd have DRDs to help me with my work. What about you? If you could choose one, which would it be?"

Any one you were in. He couldn't say that out loud, though. It might make her tuck herself back into her shell and leave him eating his sandwich by himself. "I might like to hang out with Han Solo and Chewie for a while."

"I had you pegged right. You're a troublemaker. You don't think John Crichton would be fun?" They discussed *Farscape* for a while and how several of the actors ended up on Stargate years later. Then, they argued about their favorite episodes of many of the science fiction shows and movies they'd seen.

"If it has the word 'star' in it, I've made every attempt to see it. It's not always easy to do with my father patrolling everything. What got you into science fiction?"

"My mom was a bit of a movie buff and wanted to see everything out there, so we went to the theater a lot. I just kind of veered toward the fantasy and science fiction realm. The creativity involved in that kind of storytelling is fantastical."

Tabitha bit her lip, and her eyes sparkled again. He wasn't sure why. Because they both liked similar stuff? Would that mean she'd start warming toward him? Heck, he'd discuss science fiction with her every day if it would bring them closer together.

"If your father doesn't like fantasy, how did you get to watch all this?"

"In college."

"Did you live away?" For some reason, he imagined she'd had to go local.

"I commuted to college my first year because he didn't want me being in a dorm unsupervised. Then, my grades weren't as high as he wanted, so I said that the long drive took up time I could be studying.

For the next three years, he allowed me to live at school, but I had to stay in an all-girl dorm and room with the daughter of another preacher he knew. Figured we'd keep each other out of trouble."

"Did you?"

Tabitha threw her head back and laughed. "She was a million times more rebellious than I ever thought of being. My form of mutiny was reading every book and watching every movie and show I wasn't allowed to when I lived at home. My roommate went out partying every night and often didn't come home because she'd hooked up with some guy. Exactly what my father didn't want me doing."

"And she didn't flunk out?"

"She was really smart and went to most classes, then did her work in between. Once dinner time rolled around, though, she was gone like a shot. By junior year, she'd moved in with her boyfriend. Unofficially. She still had stuff in the room we shared, but it was kind of like having my own place. I never complained because they might have put someone else in who was worse."

"Worse than a party girl?" His grandfather had paid for him to have his own apartment while he'd been in college. It had been kind of lonely at times, but he'd had plenty of peace and quiet to study, something that was required to get his tuition paid for.

"She was rarely there and didn't mess the place up. Believe me, there's far worse. Kayla had one roommate who always took her clothes, wore them without asking, then never washed or returned them. She did the same with food. One of Maggie's roommates used to bring guys over for the night. And not for watching TV, if you know what I mean. Fortunately, we were at the same school, and I had an empty bed she could use when it got a little crowded in her dorm."

"Why didn't you and Maggie just room together to begin with?"

"Maggie was in the Honors program and lived in that dorm. I wasn't smart enough, though I managed to get my grades up once my father allowed me to stay on campus. There was no way I wanted him to make me start commuting again."

"So you got three years of freedom."

Tabitha rolled her eyes. "For part of the week. I was required to come back every weekend so I could go to church at the Chapel. Dad doesn't trust any other preacher with my soul."

"It's a nice soul. I can understand him wanting to protect it. It must have been difficult to go back to living under his roof once you graduated."

Her smile dimmed. "You can say that again. I honestly thought I'd proved myself, but he started on the living-at-home-and-saving-money rant he harps on any time I even suggest finding my own place."

"I'm surprised you didn't hit up one of your boyfriends to get married. That would get you out."

"If I know my father, he'd probably want us to live with him to save money. Not that I ever had any boyfriends I could pull that on."

She couldn't be serious. "Did your father run off all the local guys, too?"

After stuffing her trash in her lunch box, she sighed. "Most guys either assumed I was too puritanical to date, so they didn't ask me, or they thought I was like my roommate, the preacher's daughter who rebelled and slept with every guy around. They never asked for dates, just hinted they'd be willing to give me a good time. No one wanted to put in the effort to get to know the real me."

Wes reached across the table and stroked his fingers over her hand. When she didn't pull away, he was encouraged. "The guys around here are idiots. The Tabitha Dailey I've gotten to know is well worth the effort."

Her cheeks turned pink, and she tugged her hand from his. "I never did properly thank you for buying me that Easter hat."

"You looked absolutely gorgeous in it. Showed up every woman in the chapel."

"Hardly, but at least I didn't feel out of place for once. Thank you for that." She got to her feet, then glanced down at him and smiled. "I don't have much on my plate for this afternoon. Do you need another hand with any of the construction?"

He eyed her skirt and blouse. "In that?"

"I've got casual clothes I can put on. I live right there." She canted her head in the direction of her house. "You got something I can work on that's more exciting than typing, farm boy?"

He nodded, and she swept up the walk to go change. She'd offered to help him of her own accord. He'd take that as a good sign.

Tabitha skipped toward her house, a feeling of excitement swirling inside. It wasn't because she'd be spending more time with Wesley. No. It was merely a nice day outside, and she couldn't stand being cooped up inside the office with nothing to do. It didn't hurt that she'd discovered Wes enjoyed science fiction and fantasy and knew enough to discuss it. Could they talk more on the subject?

As she shimmied out of her skirt and blouse and donned an old pair of jeans and a worn t-shirt, she thought of what she could ask him.

Her friends were the best in every way, except none of them were into science fiction or fantasy the way she was. There'd never been anyone to converse with regarding her favorite shows and movies.

After tugging on a pair of canvas sneakers, she ran a brush through her hair, then scowled. What was she doing? Making herself more presentable for the farm boy. Ridiculous. Supposedly she was helping him with the construction, not going on a date.

She ended up twisting her hair into a messy bun, then added some colored lip balm. To protect her lips. From the sun. Certainly not to attract Wesley Roberts. He already liked her too much.

He was pouring sand into a large bucket when she got back to the construction site.

"What can I help with?"

"You want to haul those concrete blocks over here?" His eyes gleamed with mischief.

She eyed the blocks near the edge of the lawn, then glanced at the ones lined up near where the addition was going. "Um, sure. Let me go put my superhero outfit on."

Wes chuckled. "I'm just teasing you. I've got that mini skid steer to bring them over. You can help me by stirring this mortar to keep it from setting while I start layering them."

Tabitha took hold of the stick and used all her muscles to keep it going round in the bucket. After scooping a plop of the mortar onto the block that was already there, he hefted the next one on top, fitting it into place. His muscles bunched and flexed as he shifted it to line up with the one underneath it. She hated to admit how good he looked.

"So, I just keep stirring this?"

"Bring it over here. You can use the trowel to put more mortar on the next block while I get it ready to go on top." He showed her how to scoop it up, how much she needed, and where exactly it needed to go.

It took a few tries, but his words of encouragement gave her confidence, and she soon got the hang of it.

Once they got in a rhythm, she started to chat. "You like science fiction, but how about fantasy and adventure?"

"Sure, all that's good. Marvel, DC, all the stars, Harry Potter—"

"You like Harry Potter?" She watched him closely as he guided the next block in place.

"Who doesn't?" Wes grabbed a bandana from his back pocket and wiped his forehead.

She could name one person who wasn't a fan of The Boy Who Lived. Her father. "Who's your favorite character?"

He squinted her way. "I'm surprised you didn't ask which house I'm in. That's usually the first question most people want to know."

"It's obvious you're a Hufflepuff. Hard worker, loyal, patient. That's a no brainer."

The grin he shot her way sent tremors through her. Why couldn't she resist him? She shouldn't have come out to help him. Yet, she was having a blast stirring mortar and slapping it on the foundation.

"And you're a Ravenclaw, undoubtedly."

She was, but she wouldn't give him the satisfaction of being correct. "Your favorite character?"

"Any of the Weasleys. I have a thing for red hair." His wink had those tremors double timing it. "Your favorite?"

"I like the Weasleys, too, Ron being my absolute favorite. He's completely underrated. He does so much for Harry but never gets the credit for most of it. And he's solid and true."

"Ron is a good friend to have. I bet he'd stand here, plopping mortar onto cinder block to help with an addition and never complain that it was boring."

At his words, she stood straighter. "I don't find this boring. I'm outside on a beautiful day and using my hands and body instead of typing away aimlessly on my computer." Although, if she were typing one of her fantasy stories, she wouldn't be bored. Hard to do when her father was liable to walk by at any moment.

"I appreciate the assistance. It's going faster than if I were doing it all myself."

They continued to discuss more shows that they both liked to watch as the foundation grew. It felt good to play a part in building the new addition, no matter how small. How many people could say they'd done this?

The afternoon sun lowered in the sky, and Tabitha sadly admitted she needed to go lock up the office. Wes cleaned up his tools and rinsed out the bucket.

"Thanks for the help today. It was nice having an assistant."

As she swiped her hands on the legs of her jeans, she laughed. "Your assistant for now. Once I've got this building thing under control, I think you'll have to become my assistant."

She strutted away, throwing him a last peek over her shoulder.

His grin was enormous, and he muttered, "As you wish."

Chapter Nine

*T*abitha glanced up at the tap on her door. Wesley hovered in the hall, his adorable smile plastered on his handsome face. Why did she have to find him so attractive? In any other circumstance, she'd respond to his flirting with some of her own. However, unless she wanted to be stuck in this stifling little town, she needed to push back her feelings and ignore him. Hard to do when they'd been thrown together almost daily for the past two months to organize this new addition.

"What can I do for you, Wes?" *Remain professional at all times.*

"I need to go over some of the options for siding for the addition. I know your father wanted something that matched the rest of the chapel, but I can get that effect with a few different materials. Is he around, or is it more likely you'd know what he's looking for?"

After closing down a few tabs on her computer, she rolled back her chair and pointed to the conference room. All the blueprints and detail information was in there, and the large table made it easier to spread out if needed.

While she got the binder out and unrolled the plans, Wes shut the door behind them. It wasn't like he'd try anything, so why did she feel so anxious?

He edged in close behind her and scanned the documents. That's why. He always got in her way and stood too close. It made it hard to stay aloof. Now that they'd been chatting about science fiction shows every chance they got, they'd developed a camaraderie and become good friends. However, she didn't want to lead him on romantically, since she had no plans to stick around.

Should she tell him about her writing under a pen name? What would he think? No. She wasn't ready to share it with anyone except her best friends. Most likely, he wouldn't share the info with anyone, but she didn't want to take any chances.

He placed several brochures on the table beside the plans and pointed to one. "This is the siding I think matches best. It's slightly less expensive but not quite the same shade, so we'd have to paint it, which would bump the price to a higher bracket altogether. I'm not sure your father wants to up the budget any. These are other possibilities. Take a look."

Tabitha picked up the brochures and took a few steps away from him and his alluring scent. It always put her on edge and made her think of things she shouldn't.

The huff of Wesley's sigh had her glancing up. "You okay?" she asked.

One eyebrow rose. "I get that you dislike me. I'm not sure why or what I did to annoy you, but whatever it is, I'm sorry."

What was he talking about? "I don't dislike you." Quite the opposite, in fact.

That eyebrow arched higher. "Um ... any time I try and get close to you, you run in the opposite direction."

"I'm a busy lady." Not true, but she needed some excuse.

He crossed his arms over his chest, the one she tried to avoid staring at when he wore a snug t-shirt. "Tabitha. You avoid me like the plague. I'm starting to get a complex."

"It isn't anything you did."

"So you dislike me on principal. Is it my name? The color of my hair. If I got a haircut like your father suggested, would you like me better?"

"No!" She took a small step forward as she shook her head. "If you start letting my father control you, I'll lose all respect for you. Your hair is fine, and you're a nice guy. Personable. Most people think you're fun."

His eyes clouded over. "But not you?"

How much should she tell him so he didn't think she hated him? After glancing around the room and through the window in the door, she leaned in. "Listen, farm boy, this is between us, you understand?"

A tiny grin appeared on his lips. Oh, those lips. "Sure, a secret. I can keep a secret."

"Hardly a secret but not something my father needs to hear. You promise?"

He gave a firm nod. "Got it. Something sinful, and you're going to share it with me."

He was so ridiculous she couldn't help but laugh. She bit her lip to calm down. "The fact is you're a handsome, great guy, and I like being around you. But you want to get into a relationship with me. That can't happen."

His eyes popped open, and he frowned. "Why not? Are you already married? To some secret agent man who's currently living in Russia as a spy?"

What a clown. There were times she wasn't sure if she should take him seriously.

"If only. Haven't you ever just wanted to get away from where you lived?"

"Absolutely. It's why I'm here now, instead of living in Roanoke. The city was killing me."

"Yes, and this small town is killing me. There has to be more to life than working for my father as a church secretary. I heard you say to Maggie once that you wanted to spend the rest of your life here."

His hands planted on his hips. "And that's why you won't go out with me? Because I want to stay in town?"

She nodded. "It seems easier to avoid any entanglements that would keep me here. My mother wanted more from life, but once she fell in love with my father, she had to settle for living wherever he had a congregation."

Wes narrowed his eyes. "So she wasn't happy here?"

Another sigh. "No, she was. She loved the people of this town, but she never got to do what she wanted to do. Then, she died without ever having accomplished some of her goals in life."

"What happened to her?"

"She got a burn on her hand from cooking, and it got infected. She ended up with septicemia. She didn't think it was any big deal, but by the time we got her to see a doctor, it was too late."

"I'm sorry. How old were you?"

"Mid-teens. Not the best time to lose my mom. I took over in the office once she was gone. With the exception of my college years, I've been there ever since. I don't want to spend my whole life as a church secretary. I want to see what living in the big city is like. To experience the nightlife and not roll up the sidewalks at nine PM. To travel a bit. Live my dream."

His mouth pinched. "And you can't do that here?"

Glancing around, she whispered, "I can't do it here, around my father."

Wes leaned in, and she caught his enticing scent again. "Because your dream is to be a pole dancer?"

Plopping into the chair behind her, she shook with laughter. He needed to stop being so charming. It wouldn't do to fall for him.

Chapter Ten

Wesley packed up his tools and stowed them in his toolbox. The addition was coming along well and, at two months in, was ahead of his original schedule. With the help of the kids Maggie and Donovan had hired to work the farm, he'd been able to do some of the larger sections in a shorter period of time.

Reverend Dailey strolled down the path toward his car and waved. "Thank you, Mr. Roberts, for your fine work," he called out. "Tabitha has the next check for you in the office. Looks like we'll have a new section of the chapel ready by fall."

"I'll try my best, Reverend Dailey. Do you mind if I ask Tabitha to help me with a few details for the house I'm building? She's so good at those finer points."

"By all means, ask her. I'm sure she's got most of the church business finished at this point, efficient as she is."

After loading his tools in his SUV, Wes ambled into the church offices until he stood in Tabitha's doorway. Her fingers flew over the keys, and her eyes gleamed. What was she doing to get her so excited? A tiny smile played peek-a-boo on her lips as she typed.

When he shifted in place, the door jamb creaked, and her head whipped up. She scowled. Immediately, she clicked a few more keys, pulled a flash drive from the computer, then stuffed it in her pocket.

"What do you need?" Her voice wasn't its typical professional tone.

"I'm sorry. I didn't mean to interrupt you. I'm done for the day, and your father said you'd have the next check for me."

"Of course, of course. I've got it right here." She opened the center drawer on her desk and fiddled inside.

"If you're in the middle of something important, I can get it Monday. There's no rush."

"Nothing important." Her sigh told him it was important to her but maybe not anyone else. She withdrew an envelope and held it out. "Here you go. I didn't mean to snap at you. I was just involved in what I was doing, and you startled me. I thought everyone had gone home for the weekend."

"I'm on my way. I actually wanted to ask you a favor, if you don't mind and have time."

Her chin tipped up as she waited for him to continue. The freckles across her nose and cheeks gave her that adorable innocent look he'd found so attractive in her. That and the long red hair, tied neatly in a low ponytail, had sealed the deal the second he'd met her.

"You know I just moved into my new place. It's completed enough to pass the inspections and live in, however a lot of the finishing touches haven't been added yet. Hardware, shelving, inside doors, that type of stuff. I was wondering if you'd be willing to come out and give me some tips on making it homier, finished."

"You want my opinion on your house? Why?"

"I've seen what you've done on the plans for the addition. You've got good taste."

Her eyebrow rose. "You want your house to look like a church?"

He gave a low chuckle. "Not exactly, but you've got a knack for knowing what looks good, and I'm not great at that stuff. Right now, it looks like a log cabin. I figure you can give me a female's perspective and some ideas how to spruce it up."

"You planning on having a female live there with you soon?"

Was that regret in her voice? It couldn't be. She'd turned down every advance he'd made toward her.

"I'd like to get married and have kids at some point. It doesn't have to be tomorrow, but I don't want to wait another ten years. I want the house to be acceptable to my future wife."

"I'm sure whomever you end up with will have lots to say about her new home and might want to make changes before she moves in."

"And that's fine. For now, I want the place to have a homey feel and be pleasing enough for when I have visitors. Will you help me?" He made sure to give her his most charming smile. It worked on most women, of all ages. Tabitha was the only one who'd been able to ignore it.

"When did you want to do this?" She glanced at the organizer on her desk.

"Whenever you have time. What are you doing tonight? Do you have plans with Maggie, Aubrey, and Kayla?"

Sucking in her lips, Tabitha inhaled deeply. "No, Maggie's going to her in-laws, the poor woman. The other two have to work."

"So, is tonight a good night? I saw your father going off in his car. I'm guessing he doesn't need you for anything."

"He volunteered to help the Boy Scouts in their end of year celebration ceremony. He'll have dinner there and come home later to rehearse his sermon for Sunday."

"Sounds like you might be available. Unless you wanted to listen to him rehearse."

He could tell by her expression that was the last thing she wanted to do. Her shoulders rose and fell, then she nodded.

"Okay, but I'll need to change and grab something to eat first. I get hangry if I'm not fed regularly."

"How about I pick up some takeout and we eat it at my place? What are you in the mood for? Pizza?"

One side of her mouth lifted. "If you want that."

"But you don't." He was starting to read her face and emotions easily.

After tapping away on her keyboard again, she shut down the computer. "I get together with my girlfriends every Wednesday, and we usually do pizza. There's only so much I can handle in one week."

He kept his eye on her as she locked up the desk and grabbed her purse. "Okay, what does sound good? Barbecue? Subs? Italian? Greek? Chinese?" At the last one, her expression changed. "You want Chinese?"

She shooed him out the door and locked the office behind her. "There's no Chinese place in town."

"Not in town, no, but there's one near the county line past my place."

"If your place is where you said it was, the Chinese restaurant is at least twenty minutes beyond your house."

"I'll call on the way, and the food'll be ready when we get there. Go. Put something comfortable on. I'll be in the SUV." Hovering over her most likely wouldn't get her to move any faster. The fact she'd agreed to go with him was miraculous after ignoring him for the past two years.

No more than ten minutes later, she showed up in denim cut-offs—not too short—and a navy t-shirt. Matching canvas sneakers were on her feet.

"I can follow you in my car."

Wes shook his head. "Nope, I'll drive you there and bring you back."

Her brows slid toward each other. "You don't have to drive me back. It'll be late."

Late? That gave him hope. "Which is why I'll drive you back. I have no doubt that you're perfectly capable of taking care of yourself, but the road out of my place isn't paved or even graded yet, and your car doesn't have four-wheel drive. Besides, it's more efficient for me. I poured another concrete pad today and want to come back to make sure it's setting okay. I can do that when I drop you off."

Her eyes rose to the sky, and she shook her head.

They settled in the SUV, and Wes pulled onto the road. Pointing to his phone in the cup holder, he said, "The restaurant site is on there. See what you want and send an order. You can do it online or call."

"What kind of food do you want?"

"I'm easy. As long as we get some pork fried rice and some teriyaki, I'll be good."

It didn't take her long to scan the menu and call with their order. It made him happy she didn't scrimp on the food. Too many of his dates from the debutante crowd would order a salad, then only pick at it. They had to fit in their size one clothes. Thank God, Tabitha knew how to eat and didn't seem like she'd blow away on a stiff breeze.

As they drove, they chatted about the addition for a short time, then Wes started asking some questions, wanting to learn as much as he could about this woman who had his insides twisted in a knot every time he saw her.

"Do you have any pets?"

Her jaw hardened, and he could have kicked himself. Apparently, not a good topic.

"No. My father didn't have time for one, and we had to remain frugal. Getting a pet would have cost the parishioners too much money."

"Did you want a pet? I've been thinking of getting a dog once my house is in better shape."

"I'd love a dog, though I suppose if I go live in the city, I'll be less likely to be able to have one. For now, I'd like to have a house and family someday. After I do some exploring."

It eased his mind that she wasn't opposed to the idea of getting together with someone, he assumed in union of holy matrimony. She couldn't even rebel enough to move out of her father's house, so doubtful she'd live with some guy without being married.

"What kind of dogs do you like?"

"I've never had much interaction with dogs, though I'm pretty sure it wouldn't be one of those tiny yapping things."

"Like Big Mama Prescott has?"

Tabitha snorted, then glanced away embarrassed. "Exactly. Thank goodness she doesn't bring it to church on Sundays."

"I understand she pays big money for someone to take her little princess out for a walk in her baby carriage and play with her while we're all at the service and potluck. When I heard the amount, I thought of applying for the job myself, but it's only a few hours here and there, so it wouldn't exactly pay the bills." A little baloney to keep Tabitha entertained. She laughed, so he'd been successful.

"I always wanted a collie like Lassie," she said. "It was one of the few shows my father allowed me to watch, wholesome shows with families that loved each other through thick and thin."

They pulled into the parking lot of the Chinese place. "I'll run in and grab it."

She started to dig through her purse, but he held up a hand to stop her. "We'll square later." No chance he'd let her give him any money for the meal. It was his suggestion, after all, to get the food and go to his house. She'd be doing him a favor helping him with decorating details.

When he got back, he dumped the large bag in her lap and got the vehicle moving again. "If you really can't wait until we get back, it looks like there's something on a stick poking out of the opening."

"You don't mind? My lunch was minimal today."

"Have at it. Just save me a few bites." Honestly, if she spent more time with him, he'd give up the entire meal, fried rice and all.

Tabitha had devoured a chicken teriyaki and a Crab Rangoon by the time he pulled down his driveway. As they approached his house, the food froze on its way to her mouth. Her gaze ping ponged from the house to him and back.

"You said a little cabin in the woods. This is no little cabin."

Chapter Eleven

*T*abitha couldn't believe her eyes. The house that stood in front of her was massive. Yes, it was a log cabin. By definition, it was built from logs, yet the word "cabin" hardly described the place. And the location? The yard around the house was level with a few trees dotting the landscape, then it dropped off to a small incline that led to the New River. The view of the river was spectacular.

"You made me think it was a tiny cabin. It's huge."

Wesley shrugged. "I think it just seems bigger because of the building material. It's got four bedrooms and an office alongside the regular stuff."

"Regular stuff?"

"Living room. Kitchen. Dining room. Bathrooms."

"How many bathrooms does it have?" The parish house only had one. It hadn't been fun growing up, trying to keep her feminine stuff private from her father.

"Three. One on the main floor, one upstairs, and one in the master bedroom. Come on. I'll give you the grand tour." Her stomach growled, and Wes paused. "We'll start with the kitchen."

She bundled up the bag of food and followed him inside. The entryway was two stories high with a stairway to the right that led to a bannistered balcony with doors behind it. Wes trudged straight back to an open area with counters and appliances.

"This is the kitchen as you probably figured out. The dining room is there." He indicated the empty room on the right. "I don't have a dining table yet, so we'll have to eat at the counter. I bought some high-top stools and have been sitting on them for meals."

After depositing the food on the counter, Tabitha glanced around. Some of the walls had wallboard, but a few were still exposed logs. It was definitely rustic. Still, Wes was right when he said it needed a few touches.

"I've only got paper plates at this point. I'm hoping to find time to do some shopping once I get the church addition finished."

With what he was being paid, it was likely he didn't have the money for good dishes. "The church has a rummage sale in June. You might be able to find a set then. Lots of people clean out the stuff they haven't used, or we get household items from families that are moving or have passed away."

Tossing the plates on the counter, he said, "That's a good idea. I have some utensils, so we don't have to eat with our fingers." He dug in the drawer next to the stove and grabbed a few forks and a large spoon that he stuck in the rice.

No sense waiting. She was hungry. After dropping a few appetizers on her plate, she scooped out some rice, then set it back on the counter. Wes peeked in the container and grinned.

"You left me some. Good."

Tabitha laughed, then dug in. They ate in comfortable silence for a few minutes, and she examined the room. "Do you plan on keeping the exposed logs in most of the house?"

Wes swallowed, then shook his head. "No. I think I'll keep them in the family room, but the bedrooms will be warmer with wallboard. Not to mention it'll be easier to hang things on the walls."

"I'd imagine it would be appealing to have different colors in each room. The wood color is fine, but I wouldn't want my entire house all brown."

He forked some rice in his mouth, then wiped his face with a paper napkin. "What colors would you suggest?"

"It's your house. What colors do you like?"

"I don't know. The house I grew up in was kind of sterile, white walls in every room. I definitely don't want that. This is why I need your help. Between the boring house I grew up in and the bunkhouse, I haven't had lots of examples of *Better Homes and Gardens*."

"Let me finish my dinner, and we can go through each room. I'll give you a few suggestions, then you can choose what you like."

Wes gave her a thumbs up as he had an egg roll in his mouth. Man, he was cute, even when shoveling in food. Maybe coming here and seeing his house wasn't a good idea. It gave her thoughts of domestication and family, something she eventually wanted but not until she'd had a taste of so much more.

Since Chinese food was a specialty she rarely got, she enjoyed every last bite. They packed up any of the leftovers and put them in the fridge.

"Let me wash my hands, and you can give me that tour you promised."

She ran her hand along the double basin sink. "This is gorgeous. I love the farmhouse style, yet the carved ivy pattern is so unique. Is this marble?"

"It is. It's got a small chip in the back corner, so I got it for a bargain. Does the faucet go okay with it? I wasn't sure."

"It's beautiful. I love brushed nickel because it's easy to clean and doesn't show all the watermarks or fingerprints."

His little grin caused tiny jitterbugs to dance inside her stomach. Hopefully, they wouldn't upset all the Chinese food she'd just eaten.

"Before we leave the kitchen, what would you suggest in here? Any special colors?"

She bit her bottom lip as she ran palettes through her mind. "Nothing too bright. Personally, I'm a fan of soft colors and pastels. Maybe a pale, buttery yellow or sage green. If you go with yellow, I'd accent with navy. Curtains, kitchen cannisters, tea kettle, that type of stuff."

"Blue and yellow. Sounds like a good combination. Any other suggestions for the kitchen?"

"Maybe a small cabinet to put right here." She gestured to the empty spot next to the fridge. "It'll give you more counter space and storage underneath. Not that you don't have tons of cabinets, but it's always lovely when you have room for all your kitchen gadgets, and they aren't sitting on top of each other. Every now and again, my father wants waffles for breakfast. Unfortunately, the waffle maker is way in the back of the pantry closet, underneath half a dozen other pots and pans we only use occasionally."

"I thought your father was all about frugality. What are you doing with a waffle maker?" His eyebrows waggled comically.

She rolled her eyes. "My mother was a wonderful cook and loved using kitchen gadgets. It was the one thing my father always spoiled her with, though I'd guess they got the waffle maker from the yearly rummage sale for a discounted price."

Wes indicated the connecting dining room and asked her opinion. She mentioned her favorite style of table and said he needed a hutch or sideboard or both, since the room was fairly large. "If you plan on having lots of kids, you'll need the space."

"Depends on my wife and how many children she wants." His gaze stayed on her as he said this.

Oh, no. She couldn't get pulled in with that adorable charm of his. Walking out, she said, "Show me the rest of the house."

The three upstairs bedrooms were all empty and the bathroom had the bare minimum. She suggested some color schemes that could work for now and talked about getting at least one bedroom set up in case he wanted to have visitors stay.

They worked their way back downstairs into the family room. It was a few steps down to the left of the front entryway. The sight of the floor-to-ceiling windows in the back that led to a deck had her gasping for air. When she saw a carved wooden mantle and fireplace on the left wall, she actually moaned out loud.

"This is absolutely gorgeous. The view of the river is fabulous. I could sit here and watch the water flow by all day long."

His words right near her ear startled her. "You're very welcome to."

Swirling around, she marched back to the hearth, away from him. "The furniture is a little sparse in here."

His laughter rang out in the large room. The only thing in the room was a TV and a couch. "See? This is why I need some advice. What do I need here?"

"Besides furniture?" This room had the exposed logs. It worked with the mantle and fireplace that dominated almost half of the side wall. "I'll have to think about it."

Wesley trotted up the three stairs back to the entryway. "Let me show you the other two rooms."

One of them had to be his bedroom. Did she want to be that close to the man in his private sanctuary? Yes. No. No, she definitely didn't.

The hall to the right of the door took them past the bathroom and his office. She had more suggestions when she noticed all he had was a folding table with lots of papers on it.

"Last room. Master suite. Tell me what you think. I already put the walls up because I wanted it to feel cozier in here. What do you think?"

Hovering in the doorway, she blinked at the sight. The room wasn't huge. A massive sleigh bed with unique in the headboard and footboard was placed against the far wall. Dark walnut stood out against the stark white of the walls. Wes leaned against a doorway on the right, and Tabitha could see a tub and sink within.

"I'd want to paint the walls a light color in here, or it'll be too dark."

After crossing the room, Wes pulled the curtains aside, and she gasped at the view of the river. He'd be able to see it from his bed. Wow. To keep herself from moaning again, she checked out the bathroom. The walls were bare, but he'd done a fine job picking out a whirlpool tub, shower, toilet, and vanity for the double sink.

"Some lady is going to be very lucky when she moves in here." It wouldn't be her. She had things to do and wasn't going to allow her dreams to die because of a beautiful house. Even if the house was away from her father and owned by an absolutely remarkable man. No.

"I hope she'll feel that way." His gaze never wavered.

Thinking about what he was being paid for the church addition and his previous job at Maggie's, she rounded on him. "How can you afford this? It must have cost a ton."

"I'm doing all the work myself." He shrugged but finally glanced away.

"Still. Maggie said you never took a full paycheck from her."

He cocked his head. "I lived in the bunkhouse and ate her food, so I didn't have a lot of other bills. I still earned enough to save some money, and I had some from my previous job."

He'd never mentioned much of his past. "What did you do before?"

That flirtatious grin appeared. "I wasn't a farm boy. Are you disappointed?"

"Were you a dreaded pirate?"

His face fell. "Sadly, no."

"Then I'm disappointed. I always wanted to date a pirate." Let's see what he'd do with that.

His grin returned. "So, if I became a pirate, you'd go out with me?"

"Sure, but it's kind of hard to be a pirate when we're landlocked. The ocean is several hundred miles away."

"The river's right there." He indicated the scene out the window.

"It doesn't actually lead to the coast."

Wes waggled his eyebrows. "I could kidnap you and whisk you away to the ocean and my pirate ship. You said you wanted some adventure."

She felt like playing with him. "If you do that, what happens to your house? And the church addition?"

"If I'm a pirate, I don't have to be responsible, do I?"

Her heart grew light, and she actually giggled. "I suppose not."

Chapter Twelve

*L*istening to Tabitha laugh drove away all the stress in his life. For a few minutes, anyway.

"To get you to go out with me, it might be worth it to be a pirate."

Her eyes shuttered, and she pivoted to stroll back down the hallway. He tagged along behind. They'd been getting along great lately. He'd go with her anywhere. Did she know this? The way he mooned over her at times, she had to.

In the entryway, she swiveled toward him. "You never did tell me what you used to do. Did you always work construction?"

How much did he want her to know at this point? He stepped down into the family room and stared out the back windows. "My grandfather taught me how to build, but my college degree is in business and marketing. I worked in an office for several years. I hated it. Like you hate being a church secretary. It wasn't the right life for me."

He felt her behind him, her hand touching his arm. "I'm glad you got out."

For a few minutes, they lingered there, staring out the window as the river rolled past. She'd touched him of her own volition. That had to mean something.

Finally, he twisted to peek at her pretty face. "Do you have a curfew?"

Her mouth pursed. "Of course I don't. I'm twenty-eight." She still seemed uncomfortable.

"But?"

She rolled her eyes and sighed. "Unless he knows exactly where I am, my father gets ornery when I'm out past eleven."

Wes tipped his chin in the direction of the TV set. "I've got cable and internet with several streaming services. You name the Star, and I can get it on the set."

This made her eyes sparkle with excitement. "I'll text him and let him know I'm watching a few shows with a friend. It should be good."

Her tone sounded a few moments later and she smiled, then stuck her phone in her pocket. "He's good with it, and I made sure he knows I have a ride home. He'll probably be asleep by ten."

Wes peeked at his watch. Almost eight. "We've got time for maybe two episodes if you want to do a TV show. Or one movie. What'll it be?"

"Oh, that's a hard decision. But I've gotta go with Stargate."

"SG-1 or Atlantis?"

"Let's do SG-1. It's been a while since I've watched it."

Wes guided her to the couch and pressed the buttons on the remote. The TV came on, and he scrolled through the choices. "Do you need to start from the beginning, or should we each pick an episode?"

"I've seen them enough I don't need to start at the beginning. Ooh, a favorite episode. There are so many."

"I already know what I want. 'Urgo'. Cracks me up every time."

She bounced beside him on the cushions. "That's a great one. I'll pick something that's more serious. How about 'Divide and Conquer'?"

"Why that one?"

She bit her lip and stared at the floor. "I really like the relationship between Jack and Sam in that one. They finally admit their feelings for the other."

Well, well. Tabitha was a romantic. You could never tell with how frequently she'd pushed away his advances. He could say a whole lot about his feelings for her but decided to keep it to himself. Maybe if they ever went on a date, he'd finally tell her. Not tonight.

The screen changed to the episode, and Wes dropped the remote on the floor and settled back to watch. During the initial credits, he asked, "If your father didn't allow you to watch this show, how have you seen so many of them?"

Her lips twitched. "Some in college or at friends' houses. These days I have my own laptop. At night, when he's busy, I go to my room and put in earbuds. I always make sure to have another tab open in case he happens to come in."

"Does he do that? Just walk into your room?" He hated the thought of her having no privacy at all.

"Not in a long time. He did it once when I was about eighteen, and I was getting dressed. Since then, he always knocks and then waits for me to give him the all clear."

As they watched the show, they discussed the characters and which ones they liked better. Debating which episodes were better than others was fun, and he discovered she was a huge Jack O'Neill and Samantha Carter shipper. The fact she knew a shipper was someone who liked a certain relationship on a show only made him like her more.

They got to the second episode, and she took a bathroom break. When she plopped back on the couch, she sat a little bit closer than she'd been before. No complaints from him.

By the end, their shoulders were touching, and he'd completely missed what had happened on the TV.

Tabitha stood and stretched her arms over her head. "I hate to break this up, but I need to get home. It's been fun. Thanks."

"Let me get that Chinese food, and you can take it home."

"No, you paid for it. You should keep it. I owe you for what I ate, though."

"You don't owe me anything. It would have cost me a fortune for the kind of advice you gave me tonight about the rooms. It's the least I can do. And I'll be out of the house most of the weekend, so the food will go bad if it's left here."

A gleam came to her eyes, and she nodded. "Okay, then, I'll take it. But you can keep the egg rolls. I won't eat them."

"It's a deal." He got the bag, sans egg rolls, handed it to her, then escorted her out to his car.

The ride home was more chatter about the show they'd watched and what they'd watch next time. Wes didn't even want to question her about there being a next time. Bringing it to her attention might make her take it back.

When they finally arrived at the chapel, she directed him to the parking lot instead of her driveway. "You can just leave me here. I don't want to wake my dad up."

"I want to check the concrete I poured earlier today."

"Oh, that's right." They walked past the church and stopped near the addition.

"I really appreciate all your suggestions tonight, Tabitha. Thank you." He kept his voice low so as not to wake her father.

"I'm happy to help. I'd love to see it when it's all finished."

"I'm sure I'll have more questions along the way. You could come over again to give me more input, and we could binge a few more episodes."

Her nod had him excited.

Holding the bag of food, she edged closer. She pressed up on her toes and touched her lips to his cheek. "Thanks for the takeout and the shows. But so you know, it was simply a fun night hanging with a friend. It wasn't a date."

As she scurried off into the house, his smile turned to a frown. A friend. That's all she wanted. He about faced and mumbled, "As you wish."

When Tabitha finally had a chance to get in line for food at the Sunday potluck, Aubrey, Maggie, and Kayla surrounded her, eyes narrowed.

"Word on the street is Miss Tabitha Dailey spent some quality time with a certain sandy-haired boy at his private residence Friday night. Do you deny it?" Kayla asked, her head cocked in question as she grabbed a plate and sidled behind her.

"His private residence?" Aubrey squawked, though kept her voice low to avoid any curious onlookers. "There was a chaperone, I assume. Miss Dailey would never put herself in a compromising position like that."

Maggie leaned closer, depositing a piece of chicken onto her plate. "What were you doing at the private residence of a gentleman? He was a gentleman, wasn't he?"

Tabitha sighed. It had been fun doing this kind of thing when Maggie and Donovan had first gotten together. Not so much now.

"How did you know I was anywhere Friday night?"

Kayla planted one fist on her hip. "Wesley stopped at the farmer's market yesterday and asked my mom all sorts of questions about kitchen stuff. The right kind of dishes, what kind of bakeware was best, the type of utensils someone might need when decking out cooking space. He told her you'd given him suggestions for what he could do to make his new house better. While you were in said house. Do you corroborate that you were there?"

Aubrey slid her overly large sunglasses to the end of her nose. "What else did you do whilst you were in this gentleman's abode, pray tell?"

Tabitha waved them away and scooped green bean casserole onto her plate. "Nothing. We had some takeout, he gave me a tour, and asked my opinion on what each room needed to make it comfortable and cozy."

Maggie grinned as they moved down the tables. "He wanted your opinion because he wants to make the rooms perfect for his future wife. Coincidence? I think not."

"What else did you do?" Kayla slapped one of Big Mama's homemade biscuits on her plate, then plopped a dollop of honey butter on top. She tossed biscuits onto the other ladies' plates, as well.

After scraping the last of the macaroni and cheese Mrs. Longmeyer had made and squeezing it next to her casserole, Tabitha spun around.

"Nothing. I told you. Ate. Took a tour. Watched a few episodes of Stargate."

All three of her friends glanced around at the crowd, searching for her father, no doubt. Aubrey stepped in between Tabitha and the other parishioners. "Ooh, does papa know you were watching that sinful show?"

They all laughed, knowing Stargate was tamer than most shows on TV these days.

Kayla set her plate on the table and folded her arms. Maggie and Aubrey mimicked her. "Fess up. Was there any smooching during this time?"

Heat seared across Tabitha's cheeks, and she lamented her fair skin that went along with her red hair. "During the show? Absolutely no smooching whatsoever. God's honest truth." And it was.

Maggie tapped her lips with her finger. "Hmm. She specified no smooching during the show. Does that mean smooching occurred whilst not watching the show?"

Her face must be as red as her hair at this point. "No. Well, I gave him a quick peck on the cheek when he dropped me off. That's it. And I told him it wasn't a date. I gave him some advice on his house, and we watched TV. Simply friends who had a good time together."

Maggie retrieved her plate and maneuvered to the desserts. "Yes, I thought that of Donovan, too. In two weeks, we'll be sharing a marriage bed. Cheek pecking can lead to bed sharing, you know."

As she sliced up a piece of strawberry pie, Tabitha shook her head. "Not for this girl it won't. I'm not planning on falling in love with Wesley and won't give up my plans for my future."

Aubrey pouted. "Which includes leaving us."

"I can come back and visit, or you can all come see me when I find a place in the city. It'll be like a big girls' weekend every now and then."

"It won't be the same." Kayla took the last brownie. "Maybe we should encourage this cheek pecking and see if it leads our young friend to want to stay with us in our little town."

Tabitha rolled her eyes. "Forget it. What other gossip have you got for me today? There must be something more interesting than me telling Wesley to buy a set of dishes."

They all headed to the table and took seats, Maggie next to her soon-to-be husband and Tabitha somehow squished between Wesley and Kayla. They'd never stop. Not until she moved out of town.

Surprisingly, Wes didn't say anything to her, though he did sneak peeks in her direction while they ate. Occasionally, his hand bumped into hers on the table. The warm feeling that filled her each time it happened was merely due to the heat of the day. And maybe embarrassment that she didn't keep her hand away when he reached for his napkin.

"I was chatting with Della Chavez earlier," Aubrey said after sipping her tea. Her food was almost gone. "Do any of you know her?"

"She's new in town. I've seen her in the Willow Tree having breakfast a few times." Kayla wiped her fingers on her napkin.

Tabitha shook her head. "She's originally from Prescott Hill. She was a good friend of my mother's. She moved to the city when she got married, though I believe her husband died about ten years ago."

"Right." Aubrey nodded. "She's been back a few years, taking care of her mother who was sick. She passed away last month."

Kayla deposited her empty plate on top of Aubrey's empty one. "What were you chatting about?"

"She's at loose ends and bored. She's joined the Three Oaks Country Club, but even though her husband left her with plenty of money, she isn't the type to sit around and do nothing."

"I think my father used to visit when her mother was ill and pray with her. Is she looking for a job? I don't imagine she needs the money."

Aubrey's eyes sparkled. "She used to work as a secretary at a school when her son was younger. She knows how to work in an office."

"If you're suggesting we hire her at the church office, there's barely enough work for me to do. My father won't want to spend any more money to hire someone for a position that doesn't exist."

"I think she wants to keep busy and wants to volunteer somewhere that she can be helpful."

Wesley bumped her shoulder with his. "If you allow this Mrs. Chavez to come in and help, you can teach her your job. Might make it a little easier to take some time off for other things you want to do. Ease yourself out of being indispensable to your father."

Aubrey laughed. "See, he gets it. She could be your ticket out of the church office."

Tabitha pushed her plate away, and Maggie stacked it on hers and Donovan's. "I thought you didn't want me to leave."

Aubrey sighed. "I don't want you to leave town. I never said anything about staying at your boring job forever. If you can get to the point of doing things that make you happy, maybe you won't be chomping at the bit to vamoose."

Tabitha glanced over to where Mrs. Chavez stood in conversation with Cissy Hanson. When her father wandered past, Cissy snagged his attention. Then, strangely, his face grew red, and he coughed a few times. What was going on? He never had a problem speaking with Cissy. Mrs. Chavez smiled at him, and he laughed. Actually laughed. It had been a long time since she'd heard him belly laugh that way.

When Mrs. Chavez patted his arm, her dad smiled, then stared at his shoes. Hmm. Now this was an interesting situation. Perhaps she needed to pursue the possibility of having Della Chavez join her in the office.

Chapter Thirteen

Wesley adjusted his boutonniere and peered over at his friend in the black tuxedo. "How are you feeling, Sinclair? Nervous?"

Donovan tugged on his cuffs and grinned. "Nah, excited is more like it. Having Maggie in the house while I'm next door in the bunkhouse has been a massive test of my control. After today, no more waiting."

Wes didn't know if the two had jumped their vows, however they'd been nothing but proper since they'd been together. They were great role models for the teenagers they'd taken on last year. No one could fault them.

"Ms. Magnolia is a fine woman. You're getting the best, that's for sure."

Donovan's lips pursed. "You know, when I first came to the farm, I was jealous of you."

Taken aback, Wes frowned. "Me? What for?"

"Maggie always spoke so fondly of you. Seemed you couldn't do any wrong in her eyes. I thought she was interested in you."

Wes laughed. "Doubtful. Not once you came on the scene, anyway. She couldn't take her eyes off you and constantly blushed when you were around. She also knew of my interest in Tabitha."

Donovan tipped his chin up. "How's that going?"

Wes shrugged. "We've gotten to know each other a little better. She came to my house a week ago and gave me some suggestions for colors and decorating."

The wink from Donovan was unexpected. "I'd heard about that. Maggie said you got a kiss."

"Pfftt. A kiss on the cheek."

"It's a start, Wes. Don't knock it. But remember that Tabitha is a lovely woman and my wife's best friend. Treat her accordingly. If you screw up and hurt her, I have a feeling Maggie would make me hurt you. I don't want to do that. I like having a friend around here."

Travis Beaumont, Donovan's cousin and Best Man, marched into the room. "I think it's show time soon. You sure you want to do this, cuz? There are lots of fish in the sea still to explore."

"There isn't a doubt in my mind. I've been in love with Poppy since I was a teenager."

Wes snickered at the nickname Donovan had for his intended. He'd heard it often enough, and Maggie didn't seem to mind. "Is everyone else ready?"

"Cary, Franklin, and Tyson have been escorting guests down the aisle for about twenty minutes now. Wes, how did you get the honor of escorting my lovely Aunt Bitsy to her pew?"

"I must have drawn the short straw. Here I go. See you both in a few minutes."

Wes had the honor of bringing the grandmother of the groom down to her seat, as well as Donovan's mother. She gave him a once-over but seemed to accept her escort. Finally, he was able to walk Magnolia's mother down, and the wedding could begin. He made his way to the back and located Tabitha, his partner for the day. He needed to thank Maggie for putting them together.

The music started. Acacia and Tyson began the procession, followed by Cary and Talia, then Kayla and Franklin. Wes moved into place behind them and held out his arm. Tabitha slipped her hand through his elbow and gave him a tiny smile. Before their first step, he bent and whispered, "You look stunning."

Her cheeks blushed as they slowly promenaded down the aisle. The pale green dress hugged her curves and brought out the green in her eyes. Her red hair was in some fancy style, a few tendrils of it dangling in curls around her shoulders. Would she look like this if they ever got married? Could he even dare dream of what their wedding might be like?

Once they arrived at the front, sadly, he veered to the right and Tabitha to the left as they waited for Aubrey, the Maid of Honor, to finish her procession.

The music changed, and the congregation rose to their feet. Wes bit his lip as he observed Buck, Maggie's foreman and longtime friend of her father's, in his tuxedo. Without his traditional baseball cap and jeans, the man seemed decidedly uncomfortable. Still, as he escorted a beaming Maggie down the aisle, the pride on his face was evident.

Wes paid attention as the wedding proceeded and Reverend Dailey spoke of love and commitment. He'd never seen two people more in love than this couple. He peeked over at Tabitha and found her staring at him. Was she thinking the same thing that he was?

He smiled her way, causing her to blush again. He loved her fair skin and how easily it showed her moods. He loved a lot about this woman and wished he could find the key to getting her to love him back. It wasn't something he'd tell her yet. They should probably go on a few dates before he revealed his feelings.

The minister drew the couple closer and had them repeat their vows to each other, then they exchanged rings. Once they were declared husband and wife, they kissed. Not a peck on the cheek either. A kiss showing the world they belonged to each other.

They finally got to walk back down the aisle, and Wes gladly held his elbow for Tabitha to hold. Tears welled in her eyes, yet her lips curved in a huge smile.

"Happy for your friend?"

Peering up at him, she nodded. "She deserves all the happiness she can get."

"So do you."

Tabitha smiled. However, it didn't reach her eyes. "Someday. Hopefully."

As they settled into place at the back of the church so the guests could go through the receiving line, he rubbed his thumb over the soft skin of her hand. "If there's anything I can do to help you achieve your goals, any of your goals, please tell me. You know I'll be there for you."

This time her smile was real, and she squeezed his hand. "I appreciate it, Wes. For now, let's just have a great time at this wedding."

"As you wish," he said with a wink.

The thumb stroking her hand was far too distracting and dangerous. Tabitha should really pull away. Would it be too obvious if she did? Was anyone even looking at them? Doubtful, as it was Maggie and Donovan's day. All eyes should be on the bride and groom.

Then why, for heaven's sake, was Wesley Roberts still eying her? When would the stubborn man get the message and go find another woman to pursue? There were plenty of them here today, some of them out of town friends and relatives of the groom. Wes was knocking it out of the ballpark in the handsome department in his tux. He shouldn't have any problem attracting at least one.

"You got your hair cut."

His boyish grin made her knees weak. How could she pull herself together if he turned on the extra charm today?

"I know you said not to, but I figured for Maggie and Donovan's wedding, I should look half decent."

"You clean up okay for a farm boy."

His grin grew until his face beamed. Could he turn it off for a while? She'd need a defibrillator if her heart raced any faster.

"That dress is nice and looks perfect on you. Did Maggie pick it out, or did you have a choice?"

"Maggie chose the color, then allowed us to each get a dress that fit our body type." Tabitha had loved the soft sage green and had tried on a number of dresses. This one had a surplice top that hugged her curves and showed just a touch of her cleavage, then flowed around her hips and stopped an inch below her knees. Loose cap sleeves fluttered in the breeze, exposing her upper arms. Her father would never want her buying a dress like this—it showed her figure too much—but she could easily argue it was too frivolous to keep it in her closet and not wear it again. It was a perfectly acceptable dress for Sunday service. Many of the congregation wore far more revealing outfits.

The small fascinator clipped to the side of her head was another accessory Maggie had picked out, knowing Tabitha could wear it again to church. The tiny hat with matching mesh had a dozen thin ribbons wound in a bow with a few feathers in the middle. It gave just the right touch to her fancy updo. Her three-inch heels made Tabitha feel like a model. Dainty and beautiful, they highlighted her trim legs and accented the dress perfectly.

"Will you save a few dances for me at the reception?"

"We're partnered together, so we'll have to do at least one." Tabitha wasn't sure being in Wesley's arms was a good idea.

"Excellent."

The receiving line finally wound down, and they strolled to the three limousines Donovan had gotten to take them to the reception. The bride and groom slid into one with the wedding party split between the other two. Disconnecting from Wesley's arm, she attempted to get into a different car than him. He was having no part of it and guided her into the vehicle closest and snugged up right next to her to allow others to fit in.

Chatter along the way kept Tabitha from having to speak directly to the adorable man at her side, though his presence was affecting her equilibrium and throwing her off balance. Or perhaps it was simply too warm with all the people. Yes, that was the reason she felt off-kilter. Too hot in the close quarters.

"I can't wait to see Bitsy's reaction at how we decorated the new barn for the reception." Kayla beamed at Aubrey who had worked with her. Tabitha had focused on making the chapel beautiful for the wedding, while Aubrey and Kayla had gotten a team and worked on the barn.

Aubrey rolled her eyes. "Even if the place is good enough to be in a decorator magazine, Bitsy Beaumont-Sinclair won't like it because it's not the country club."

Wes tipped his head. "Didn't you get the tables, chairs, and dishes from the country club?"

Kayla nodded. "That was a concession Maggie made so Bitsy wouldn't go completely off the rails when she found out they weren't doing it at Three Oaks. I like the barn, and you should see all the stuff Aubrey made just for the wedding. I've never seen anything so amazing."

Once they got inside, Tabitha had to agree. Yards of sheer white fabric hung from the rafters draped in waves across the large area. Fairy lights crisscrossed with them, flickering in the dark space. The tables were round with lace tablecloths and linens, but the centerpieces were extraordinary.

"Is each table different?" Wes asked as they milled around inside.

Aubrey had a secret smile that showed how pleased she was at the positive reactions she was getting from everyone. "The tables all have a thin wooden ring on the bottom, but each table is slightly different."

It was like a fairy world. The centerpieces had a combination of either small metal milk cans, mason jars, painted bottles, or lanterns surrounded or filled with dried flowers. And as Aubrey said, each table was slightly different.

The rest of the room was decorated with hay bales, wooden crates, more lanterns, and an old ladder all topped with flowers, greens, and candles. An old window frame had pictures of Maggie and Donovan at different times. Tabitha was surprised to see one from when they were teenagers.

"Where'd you get this picture? I'm surprised Bitsy allowed her son to be photographed with the peasants."

Aubrey laughed. "Mrs. Mancini gave me a copy. Said she had it in an old photo album and came upon it recently. Thought I might like it for the newlyweds."

Wes bent down to take a peek, then twisted to peer at her. "Is that you in the background?"

Color rushed to Tabitha's face as she squinted at the picture. Oh, no. She'd been all arms and legs back then. "You don't need to study that picture. It's Maggie and Donovan's day. Let's go see where they want us."

For almost an hour, the wedding party and family took turns posing for the photographer while everyone else mingled and had appetizers. Wes appeared at her side and held up a plate with bruschetta and a few meatballs.

"I snagged a little snack to get us through."

Tabitha snatched the toothpick and speared a meatball, devouring it in seconds. "You are my hero."

"Did you want a drink? I can go get you something."

A glance back told her the photographer was winding down. Sure enough, the wedding party was introduced to the crowd a few minutes later, and they were able to sit and enjoy the fabulous meal.

"This food is excellent," Wes said in between bites of tenderloin and steamed vegetables.

"It's all fresh from Popham Farm. Maggie made sure the chef used her produce." Kayla held up a tiny tomato.

Tabitha nodded. "Chef Dupre uses Popham Farm almost exclusively now for the meals at the Prescott Inn. Maggie was thrilled to get his endorsement and even happier that he agreed to cater the wedding."

The music started shortly after, and the bride and groom got up to do their first dance. Once they'd made a few turns around the room, the bridal party was invited to join them. Wes held out his hand and Tabitha had no choice but to take it. If she left him standing there, it would be extremely rude, something she was taught never to be.

Unfortunately, Wesley's arms around her, even loosely, set off fireworks in her belly. She didn't understand her reaction to this man's touch. It had never happened before with anyone else, though she hadn't had many dates in the past. No one wanted to take out the pastor's daughter and risk incurring the wrath of Reverend Dailey if they didn't treat her right. She'd had a few in college, but she usually preferred to spend her free time reading books or watching shows she hadn't been able to while living at home.

Throughout the next few hours, she and Wes seemed to dance together a lot. Sometimes he'd ask, but often Maggie had special things the wedding party all had to do together. It threw her and Wes together more often than she wanted.

Liar. You like being with him. He's funny and intelligent and a pleasure to be with. As he quickstepped with her in his arms yet again, Tabitha glared at Maggie's back, then faced Wes.

"Did you put her up to this?"

His eyebrow rose. "Up to what?" He was either a great actor or innocent.

"Pushing us together so much today."

"Me? No. As much as I want you to go out with me, I'd never want you to do it against your will. When you fall deeply in love with me, it has to be your decision."

A laugh escaped her mouth. "Delusional much?" Or maybe she protested too much.

His arms tightened as they glided across the floor. "If you're gonna dream, dream big." His cute face had her in a spell. She needed to break it.

"Except you can't always control who you fall in love with."

"Exactly." He twirled her around. "That's what I'm counting on."

Chapter Fourteen

*W*es knew Tabitha was taking her break. It was like a sixth sense around her. It also helped that he could see into her office from his position next to the addition. Whatever it was, he decided to take his break, too.

Wandering over to the live oak tree, he dropped to the ground, dug his sandwich and magazine from his cooler, and leaned back to rest. He'd had the kids helping him with a good deal of the addition every so often, but now that it was June, there was a lot of farmwork to do.

As he took a bite of his sandwich, Tabitha strolled out, her own lunch bag in hand, and glanced his way. Would she join him like she had a few times a week for the past three months or ignore him as had been her way before he started working here?

Her feet brought her his way, and he smiled. Baby steps. If she just kept taking baby steps toward him, maybe they'd have a relationship yet. He could wait.

"Pull up a few blades of grass and have a seat." He patted the ground next to him. Surprisingly, she lowered herself to that exact spot. Her gaze examined the magazine he'd taken out.

"Have you read that yet?" She touched the cover. It showed a spaceship cruising through space.

"*Galaxia*? I read it every month when it comes out. I have the whole collection back at my place. For the past six years, anyway. It's got some good stuff in there."

Her eyes twitched as she stared. "What do you like best in it?"

He took another big bite, then set his sandwich in his cooler before he picked up the magazine. "They publish some really great stories in here. Most of them aren't more than a few thousand words, but some of these authors are excellent."

She searched the sky, then the area around them. Was she checking to make sure her father wasn't anywhere nearby? "Are there any authors who stand out more than others?"

He held up the magazine. "Have you read any of the stories in here?"

"I have. I usually donate mine to the library once I read them. Get rid of the evidence so to speak."

"Do you have a favorite author?"

"I have a few, but you didn't answer my question."

"I've honestly been following the stories of this one author. Tempus Elgato. Really cool stuff. The world building is unbelievably detailed and complex. Unique. Yet the storylines are simple."

A secret smile crossed her face, and he wondered if she enjoyed the works of Elgato, also. "I've read those stories, too."

"This is an older issue from last year, but it has a few really excellent stories in it. Elgato hasn't come out with anything new lately."

Casually flipping through the pages, Tabitha paused a few times to look at stuff. "Did you like this story?" She pointed to the Tempus Elgato story on the page.

"This one and all of his others."

"It wasn't too out there?"

"Not at all." Wes thought back to the story and ran it through his mind. "The author really created an incredible world in so few words. I could almost see a bunch of these stories interacting with each other to create one big universe. This guy is an excellent writer."

With her arms crossed over her chest, she leaned back against the tree. "How do you know it's a guy?"

The question surprised him. "I don't. Just assuming. It could be a woman."

Her eyes gleamed. "I'll bet it is."

She seemed awfully smug. "Why do you say that?"

"I know these things."

Scooting around, he faced her. "You know something, don't you? Do you know the actual author? Obviously, Tempus Elgato isn't their real name."

Her shrug was too casual. "Why wouldn't it be?"

He narrowed his eyes as he examined her face for clues. "Really? Tempus Elgato? His or her parents should be shot. Do you know something I don't?"

Her lips curled. "Maybe I do."

"Really? I would kill to meet this author in person. Who is it?"

"I said maybe I knew them. Maybe I don't." She reached for her lunch and took another bite.

"Now you're being coy. That isn't like you. You're usually straight-forward and direct. What do you know about Tempus Elgato?"

"Tempus Elgato writes fantasy science fiction stories."

"Really, Sherlock? That's all you can come up with for now?"

"This person lives in Virginia."

"Now we're getting somewhere. What part of Virginia? Have you actually ever met the author?"

She wiped her hands on a napkin. "We've been in the same place at the same time before."

"Like at a conference? Comic Con?"

Her eyebrows slid together. "Do you really think my father would approve of a trip to Comic Con?"

"I guess not. Are you planning to tell me who this Tempus Elgato is? I'm dying here."

"Which story did you like best?" She thumbed through the pages, returning to Elgato's story again.

"In this issue? There were a few of them, but Elgato's stories are always the most exciting by far."

"Is there one of Elgato's stories you like more than the others?"

"Why are you asking?"

"Just curious." She thumbed through the pages again. "I wondered if it would be like our favorite Stargate episodes where your favorite is very different from mine."

"Okay. I'd have to say I really loved the story when he, or she, first introduced the Kloss Nebula and the space port that services it. It's such a great location and has an interesting variety of species and alien life forms. It seems like most of the stories revolve around the comings and goings of this space station. What do you think of the Kloss Nebula? Or do you like the stories that take place on Akiva?"

Tabitha stared at the sky for a few moments, her lips pinched to the side. "Have you ever thought Akiva might be in the Kloss Nebula?"

Wes sat up straight and pointed his finger at her. "I've been mulling that around in my head, too. The bootlegger who was in the last story had some of the same qualities of the Akivans. You picked it up, too? I wonder if that's where the story is going."

As she picked up her sandwich, she shrugged. "How would I know?"

Leaning closer to her, he gazed into her eyes. "You said you know who Tempus Elgato is, so maybe you know what they're planning to do with the next story."

"I never said I know the author."

"But you know they live in Virginia, and you've been in the same location as them. Why won't you tell me who it is? I promise I won't say anything to anyone. Most of my friends aren't that into science fiction, anyway. You're one of the first people I've been able to talk to about it. It's kind of nice."

Her cheeks turned pink, and she licked her lips. "I like talking about it with you, too. As long as my father doesn't hear us."

"So tell me who it is."

She shook her head and started to rise.

"Why not?"

Peeking over her shoulder at him as she walked away, she said, "A woman's got to have a few secrets."

Chapter Fifteen

*I*t was just about lunch time. Tabitha glanced at Della Chavez, who was updating some of the parishioner files.

"Mrs. Chavez, can you handle the phones if I take my lunch break?"

"Of course, darlin'." Her soft southern accent floated across the room. "You run along and go see what that handsome man is doing outside. Maybe he wants to take his break at the same time."

Had she and Wes been that obvious in taking their lunch breaks together? "I suppose I should see how he's coming along. Dad did put me in charge of making sure the addition stayed on schedule." She'd been watching Wes climb up and down the ladder to the roof all morning long. To make sure he was safe. Certainly not because his jeans hugged his slim hips and long legs. She would never confess to the sin of lust, even if she did enjoy watching him.

Della had been training with her most of the week for three or four hours each day. They'd told her father she was simply looking for odd jobs to help out in the parish, but Tabitha was slowly introducing her to every aspect of the church secretary position. In case there ever came a time she could ease out and run.

"You know what to say if—"

"Reverend Dailey is out of town at a conference and won't be back until Saturday," Della interrupted. "If it's an emergency, Reverend Nguyen from the Baptist church is available, and I'm to give them his number. Any other calls, I take a message if I can't answer the question myself."

Tabitha grinned. The woman was efficient. "Thank you, Mrs. Chavez. I won't be long. It's just such a beautiful day today. I can't imagine eating inside."

"And you need to check on the new addition." The woman's smile said she knew exactly why Tabitha was eating outside, yet she didn't seem to be judging.

After grabbing her lunch bag, she pushed the door open and strolled across the grass. Wes swiveled toward her, then glanced at his watch. In seconds, he was on the ground, plopped next to her with his lunch bag and whatever edition of *Galaxia* he'd brought today.

Tabitha was having a blast talking about Tempus Elgato's stories with him. It was the first time she'd ever been able to discuss what she'd written and find out other people's opinions on her writing. Someday, she'd tell him it was her pen name, but she wasn't ready yet.

As Tabitha munched on her pasta salad, Wes thumbed through the magazine. "This right here is the episode I was telling you about. Where Sappho Rueb describes her home planet. When she mentions the Angrabodian Dragon leather and how it's fireproof, it reminds me of when Vared Dubrok, from the story we read Tuesday, was talking about the security factors he'd put in place to keep the Isilki out. Doesn't it sound similar?"

Tabitha wanted to jump up and shout, then kiss his beautiful lips that said such wonderful words about her stories. Instead, she kept her voice neutral. "I think you have a good argument. It would definitely be something to keep in mind as you reread the other Elgato episodes. Could be more than just those two are related."

Oh, how she wished she could tell him all the episodes were related and one day she wanted to weave them all together into the most epic story of all. One great, big action adventure and fantasy novel.

They talked about the story he'd picked today as they ate, and too soon it seemed they needed to get back to work. Well, she didn't, seeing as was Thursday and she'd finished everything on her list yesterday before she'd left. With Mrs. Chavez here, things had gotten done much quicker. On the other hand, her father wouldn't expect Wes to hang about all afternoon kibitzing about a fantasy world in another galaxy.

"Thanks for the little respite from a grueling job." He hefted himself to his feet and trudged back to the metal ladder he'd been working on. The roofers were coming next week, and Wes still had a bit more to do there before they could start. His work today did seem grueling, and it probably didn't help that he was working in full sun.

Tabitha kept her eyes on him as he climbed the rungs. He'd gotten about three quarters of the way up when she noticed a board that had been resting on the roof started to slide from the movement of the ladder. He wouldn't be able to see it from his vantage point.

"Wes! Watch out!" she yelled.

He twisted, then peered up to where she was pointing. The board descended straight toward his head. When he shifted to avoid being hit, the ladder swayed to the side. Barely hanging on, Wes tucked into a ball. Her sigh of relief was short lived as he plummeted to the ground, the ladder and board following behind.

Rushing over to him, she was too late to keep him from being hit. She pushed the board and ladder out of the way as Wes shook his head and opened his eyes. "Ow."

"Don't move. I'll call an ambulance. You've got a wicked cut on your forehead."

Wes reached out and took her hand before she could leave. "I'm fine, Tabitha. Just a little banged up."

When he closed his eyes and grimaced, she wasn't sure what to do. Mrs. Chavez teetered out on her high heels with her cellphone in her hand. "I saw what happened. Do I need to call a doctor or rescue squad?"

Arms pushing himself up, Wes took a deep breath in and slowly released it. "I'm good. I'm good. I think. Head hurts a bit." He touched his head, and his fingers came away bloody.

"You've got a good-sized cut there. It's starting to swell."

Mrs. Chavez stuck her fists on her shapely hips and pursed her lips. "Now listen here, young man. You need to let a medical person take a look at that head. You could have a concussion or some sort of brain injury."

"I'm sure ..." Wes attempted to stand but swayed between them. Tabitha glued herself to his side.

"What were you saying?"

His eyes opened and closed a few times, and his arm held her tight. Though with Wesley, she wasn't sure it wasn't just a ploy to hold her.

"The Urgent Care Center next town over on Creek Village Road takes walk-ins," Mrs. Chavez informed them. "Why don't you drive him over there, Tabitha, and I'll hold down the fort here?"

Wes appeared as if he'd object again, but then took a step and winced. "Okay, maybe that's not a bad idea. If you don't mind, Tabitha."

They both helped Wes into the front seat of her sedan, since it was easier to park than his SUV, then Tabitha gave Mrs. Chavez a quick rundown of what needed to be done and how to lock up the offices.

"I don't know if I'll be back before closing time, especially if I need to take him home and get him settled afterward."

"It's all good here, darlin'. You take care of that sweet boy and don't worry your little head about anything at the chapel. Pretty sure you have a tendency to finish off the entire week's work by Wednesday."

Tabitha chuckled, knowing it was true.

In the vehicle, Wesley had his eyes shut, so she tried not to slam the door too hard. "How are you feeling? I can still call an ambulance if you want."

Wes slid his hand along the seat and tapped hers. "It'll be quicker if you drive me. I'm sure I'm fine, but it's not a bad thing to be cautious. I am a little dizzy."

Tabitha drove quickly but carefully and got there in less than twenty-five minutes. Another reason living in a city was better. The hospital was right there. What if his accident had been even worse?

They walked in together, Tabitha under Wesley's arm, holding his waist. After giving the receptionist his name and reason for being there, they dropped into a couple of chairs by the window.

When it was his turn, Wes tugged on her hand and insisted she come back with him. "I'm not sure I'll remember what they tell me to do. My head's a little fuzzy."

No one said anything, so she toddled along beside him. Vitals were taken, his cut cleaned up, and medical history plugged into the computer. Soon, the doctor was in, poking and prodding and asking lots of questions.

"I'd say you have a slight concussion. I don't think we need to send you to the hospital, but you will need to take it easy for a few days. You should have someone stay with you for at least the first forty-eight hours. We've got a list of red flags to watch out for, as well as a list of what you shouldn't do. Screen time is the first no-no."

The nurse came in a few minutes later with the release paperwork and instructions on what to do if certain symptoms cropped up or got worse. Wes gently nodded, then handed them to Tabitha.

Once they got to his place, she ran around the car to get the door for him.

"I'm not an invalid. I just have a little headache. If you need to head back to the office, I'll be fine. I can find a way to get my car at another time."

She waited until she'd gotten him into the family room and onto a couch, then planted her hands on her hips. "I'm not going anywhere for a while. The doctor said you had to have someone with you for at least a few days. If there's someone else you want to come sit with you, let me know and I'll call them."

"No one else I'd rather have with me than you." His grin was a little off, and his eyes squinted with the bright light. Digging the paper from the clinic out, she read through it again. *Keep the lights dim. Noise to a minimum.*

"How about we get you into your bedroom? It'll be darker in there with the curtains."

"Why, Miss Dailey, I didn't think you had it in you."

As she helped him off the couch, she scowled. "You need rest, you twit. It's too bright in here. Let's go."

After getting him stretched onto the bed, she removed his work boots and fluffed up his pillows. "Is there anything else I can do? Is there someone I should call? Your parents? Siblings? Girlfriend?"

Wes snagged her hand and tugged until she perched on the edge of his bed. "I'll address that last first. Do you think I'd be asking you out so often if I had a girlfriend?"

She rolled her eyes. "Some guys would."

"Not me. I had hoped you knew me better than that by this point. As for siblings, no. I'm an only child, and I don't want to bother my parents with this. They both have very busy lives and live a few states north of here. It's hardly life threatening, and I don't want to worry them needlessly."

"You're sure? I'd want to know if it was my child."

"That's because you're a sweet, loving person."

"Your parents aren't loving? I don't believe that. You're such a nice guy, you must have had parents who treated you well."

What did she really know about Wesley Roberts? Lots about who he was and what he did now, but not much about his past. Except that he hadn't been a pirate. Too bad.

Wes wiggled on the pillows, then stroked the hand he still held. "Yes, my parents love me and are good people, but they lead very different lives than I currently want to live. My dad is an accountant for a large firm, and my mother works in corporate law."

"So who taught you how to build? Did you say your grandfather? Which one?"

"My dad's father. He was a contractor and used to take me with him from the time I was old enough to pick up nails and small scraps of lumber. I learned from the bottom up. At first, it was just cleaning up the debris, but then he started teaching me how to install wallboard, spackle and sand, then do other finish work. As I got older, he had me building the frames and walls, then learning plumbing and electrical work."

"But you said you got a degree in business. Whose idea was that?"

Wes chuckled, then grimaced and shut his eyes for a moment. "Not my idea. My parents and my mom's father convinced me it was prudent to get a degree I could use. My mother said even someone who owned their own construction company should know how to run it. I bought it and then spent six years doing something that didn't make me happy. I happened to see Maggie's ad for a farmhand and figured I'd apply and see what happened. It worked out for everyone involved once her father passed away. My business degree helped a bit, but mostly my ability to renovate some of the buildings was what she really needed."

Tabitha squeezed his hand. "Maggie always said you were a godsend when you showed up."

"I was in the right place at the right time. Not today, however. That was careless of me to have left that board on the roof. I should go back and make sure all my tools are picked up and the area is cleaned so no one else gets hurt."

"You aren't going anywhere. Let me make a call, and we'll get someone to go get your stuff together and put away."

"Who—?"

"I'll call Maggie, and I'm sure one of her crew will go take care of things. You have to rest. Is there anything you need before I make that call?"

"What if I said I needed you?"

Chapter Sixteen

Wes waited to see Tabitha's reaction to his words. Would she take them seriously or brush them aside like she'd done so many other times?

She rolled her eyes. "You don't need me."

Testing her, he said, "Then, you can head home."

Her lips pursed. "Well, maybe you need me for a few days. Just so you don't get into any trouble."

"Me? Trouble?" He added the boyish grin he'd been told was adorable.

Tabitha laughed softly. "Yes, you. If someone isn't here to make sure you rest, I have a feeling you'll be painting the unfinished rooms or adding molding to the kitchen windows."

"You noticed those weren't done, huh? I'll have to move them up on my list."

"You aren't to even think of that list for at least the next two days. I'll go call Maggie, then get you something to drink."

"It's a little early for a beer, don't you think?" He grinned as he burrowed deeper into the mattress.

The look she threw him was straight out of the mother's book of discipline. He watched as she swished out of the room, then closed his eyes. Was she seriously going to stay here for a few days? It had been his dream for the past few years, but he'd never want her to compromise herself. Lord, that was old fashioned.

It wasn't long before she sauntered back in, a glass of water in one hand and the packet of painkillers the doctor had given them in the other.

"How's your head feeling?" She placed the water on the bedside table and planted her gorgeous bottom on the edge of the bed again.

As much as he wanted her to stay and fuss over him, he wanted Tabitha to be with him because she liked him and enjoyed his presence. Not because he was hurt.

"It's okay. I'm starting to feel some of the muscles I twisted when I fell though."

Her head swiveled toward the bathroom. "You've got a jacuzzi tub, right? Might be good for you to soak in some warm water for a bit."

His eyes gleamed. "You going to help me into it?"

Her lips flatlined. "No, but I will get the water running and set up some towels. I imagine it'll take a while to fill it up. Get some rest, and I'll let you know when it's ready."

Wes didn't have the energy to object. The thought of the jets working on some of the injured muscles sounded perfect. Closing his eyes, he tried to keep the image of Tabitha in his jacuzzi with him out of his mind. A shame she hadn't offered to join him.

He must have dozed off because Tabitha gently shook his shoulder and whispered, "Wes, did you want to get into the tub?"

As he attempted to sit up, his muscles screamed and his head throbbed. She assisted him and swung his feet to the floor. "Do you need help getting in?"

Though he'd love to have her do that, her anxious expression made him find the strength to stand by himself. He wouldn't put her in an uncomfortable position.

"I think I can manage." He glanced at his watch and realized it had been five hours since they'd eaten lunch. "Would it be possible for you to make something for dinner? I'll be getting hungry soon." That should keep her busy and away from his bathroom.

Her face showed relief. That she wouldn't have to see him removing his clothes? Was she that horrified by the thought of him or merely innocent enough to be scandalized? He'd bet on innocent. She was a preacher's daughter, after all.

"Is there anything special you'd like?"

"Whatever you want to make. I went grocery shopping a few days ago and stopped at the Popham farmstand yesterday on my way home. There should be plenty of food."

He hobbled to the bathroom and gave her a smile as he shut the door behind him. The tub was filled to the brim and a few towels sat on the counter. After shucking his clothes, he eased into the water and tapped the button to turn the jets on.

Oh, yes. Just what he needed.

His eyes drifted closed again as the pain pills began to dim the discomfort. How long he stayed there he wasn't sure, but at some point a tap came on the door.

"Are you okay in there? Just making sure you didn't drown."

"Not yet."

"Um ... supper's just about ready if you want. Or I can keep it warm if you need to stay in longer."

The water had cooled considerably, though the jets still felt nice. With water splashing along the edges, he pushed himself up and snagged the towel. "I'll be out in a minute. Thanks."

"Do you need help?" Her voice seemed shaky. What would she do if he said yes? No, he couldn't put her in that kind of position.

He pulled the plug to drain the water, then wrapped the towel around his waist. "I'm good. Fair warning, I'll be coming out in only a towel. My clothes are dirty from this morning's construction." That should give her enough time to skedaddle from his room.

He rubbed his skin dry and ruffled a towel through his hair, figuring she'd have enough time to leave. However, when he opened the bathroom door, she stood at the bedroom door with it half closed.

"Did you want a show?" he teased as he stepped into the bedroom.

"Just making sure you made it all right," she called out as she tugged on the door behind her.

Wes laughed at how quick she'd made her escape. As fast as he could with his aching muscles, he donned a worn t-shirt and a pair of gym shorts. It was too hot to wear more than that.

The smells from the kitchen made his mouth water. "What did you make?"

"Chicken and broccoli Alfredo. I hope you like that. You had all the ingredients."

"You say that like you're surprised." He eased onto his stool at the counter.

Placing one plate in front of him and one at the space beside it, she tipped her head. "I guess I don't expect men to have much interest in cooking. I know that's probably sexist and old-fashioned, but you have to understand who I grew up with. Either my mother or I have always cooked for my father. Not sure who he'll get to do it once I'm gone."

"You plan on leaving soon? Where are you going?"

"Away from this little town."

"Oh, that's right. The pole dancing."

She swatted in his direction. "Eat before it gets cold."

He dug into his food and closed his eyes as the flavor exploded on his tongue. "This is delicious. I had the ingredients to make this?"

She nodded.

"Your dad better get in tight with Chef Dupre if you plan to leave town. I don't imagine there's anyone who cooks better than this."

The blush on her cheeks made her appear even more innocent than usual.

"Thank you for taking me to the doctor's and bringing me back here. It looks like you made enough of this fettuccine that I'll have some for a few more meals."

They finished eating, and Wes carried his dishes to the sink. Before he could rinse them, Tabitha came up behind him and tapped his arm.

"I've got this. You're supposed to be resting."

"I took a nap this afternoon for a bit and pretty sure I dozed off in the tub."

"Then, sit on the couch and relax. I'll join you in a few minutes."

True to her word, it was only a few minutes before she plopped next to him on the couch. "I like the new furniture you got in here. You took my advice about a lot of the stuff we discussed a month ago."

"Yup, there's a nice big desk in my office now and a bedroom set in one of the upstairs bedrooms."

Her eyes slammed shut in relief. "Oh, good. I was afraid I'd have to sleep on the couch tonight."

"Tonight? You plan on staying here?"

Her arms crossed over her chest. "You heard the doctor. You need someone with you for the first forty-eight hours. You're out in the middle of nowhere here, Wes."

"I didn't expect you to take on the responsibility of babysitting me. I'm sure I'll be fine."

Tabitha shook her head. "If there's someone else you want with you, then I'll call them. If not, I'm your gal."

In his dreams she was. As for someone else to stay with him, he didn't want to bother anyone. He and Donovan had grown closer over the past year, but the man had literally just returned from his honeymoon yesterday. The rest of the farmhands had been stretched thin with Maggie gone for a few weeks, so it was unlikely they'd want to watch him.

"Are you sure? Don't you have responsibilities at the church office?"

"With Mrs. Chavez there, my workload is almost non-existent. She's picked up how to do everything super fast."

"And your father is okay with you having a sleepover at my house?"

Her face hardened. "My father is currently away at a conference for several more days. I'll be sleeping in your spare room, so there's no impropriety. Plus, we're not going to tell him. Are we?"

Wes chuckled at the fierce expression on her face. "I won't say a word. Can't vouch for Mrs. Chavez when you tell her you can't come into work tomorrow."

Tabitha leaned back casually on the cushions. "I've already spoken with her. I made it sound like you had someone else with you at night, but I needed to come over during the day to check on you. She completely bought it. And if she didn't, she won't tell my dad because she was the one making sure you had another person with you for a couple days."

Tabitha got up and tidied the room, then bustled about in the kitchen for a bit. When Wes couldn't stand it any longer, he tugged on her hand to sit next to him.

"Stop hopping all over the place. Sit there and keep me company. I don't need you cleaning my house. Slow down and relax."

After slipping off her shoes, she tucked her feet under her. "You call it relaxing; my father would call it being lazy. Yet another deadly sin. Sloth."

Wes laughed. "I can't imagine you ever break any of the Seven Deadly Sins."

Her lips turned up at the sides. "You'd be surprised. I should probably make sure the bed upstairs is all set."

"It has clean sheets on it. I put them there when I got the set a few weeks ago. Assuming you truly plan to stay here overnight, do you need to run home and get extra clothes?"

Her tongue poked out and skimmed across her bottom lip. "I have some things in the trunk of my car. Jeans, a few t-shirts, some old sneakers."

"Is that in preparation for a quick escape if you ever get the chance?"

She laughed. "Not exactly an escape. It's in case I'm somewhere that my plain Jane dress would be ridiculous. Which is most of the places I go."

"You always look nice, Tabitha. Even in a plain dress. Your beauty shines through."

Her cheeks flushed, and she stared at the floor. "I've got stuff for tomorrow, but tonight ..."

"I can probably be persuaded to let you borrow a t-shirt of mine. It'll be kind of big, but most likely comfortable."

"That would be great. Thanks. If you're all set for now, I'll run out to my car and grab my emergency bag."

"Go. I'm fine." And he was, but once he got a peek at her in his t-shirt, he wasn't sure he'd stay okay.

Chapter Seventeen

*T*abitha woke earlier than usual the next morning, having slept in a strange bed. Extremely comfortable but not hers. Glancing around the room, she visualized what she would do in here if the house was hers. But it wasn't, and it wouldn't be. Wes was a super great guy, but she needed to get out of this town and away from her controlling father. The fact a twenty-eight-year-old woman had to keep from her father that she stayed here to help a friend was reason enough.

It wasn't like they'd done more than read and talk. Well, she read, and they both talked, discussing the Elgato stories that she read to him, since he couldn't do anything with a screen. It had been even better than the lunches they'd shared the past few weeks.

As she slipped out of bed and used the bathroom off the hallway, she chuckled at how she'd pretended to analyze the characters and plots with him, something she'd obviously done prior to actually writing them.

She dug in her bag for new clothes and quickly peeled off the t-shirt Wes had loaned her. Once dressed, she padded downstairs and got a pot of coffee brewing. Wes had a to-go cup with him every morning, so she knew he liked the beverage. Mostly black with the tiniest splash of milk or cream. No sugar. In her estimation, the man was sweet enough. Maybe too sweet. It was one of the reasons she had such a hard time keeping herself from falling for him.

But she would. There was no room in her life for someone who wanted to stick close to this suffocating town.

With the coffee percolating, she wandered down the hall and peeked into the master bedroom. The door was ajar, so it was easy to see Wes was still asleep, a long lock of hair flopped over his forehead. Her fingers itched to push it back. *Nope. Don't go there.* Dangerous territory.

The door to his office was also open, and she peered inside to check out the new desk he'd bought. It was huge and took up half the back wall. A long high table with a stool next to it was arranged on the left side of the room. Papers were scattered all over it.

She was being nosy, but they looked like drawings. Of what? As she drew closer, she gasped in surprise. The sketches held space cities, alien fantasy creatures, and incredibly beautiful dragons guarding a cave in the mountains. She pushed aside a few of the top ones to gaze underneath. Holy comic books. These were unbelievable. Some of them seemed familiar.

"Do you like them?"

The deep voice behind her made her jump and spin around. Wes grinned and tipped his chin toward the table.

"I'm sorry. I didn't mean to snoop. They just caught my eye, and I was drawn in. Did you do these?"

"I did. I'm just fooling around with them. They weren't meant for anyone to see, but it's okay that you did. What do you think?"

Tabitha shook her head. "They're out of this world. Literally. Did you model these after some of the Elgato characters?"

The gleam in his eyes got her excited. "Why? Do any of them seem familiar?"

She shuffled through a few and picked up one of the sheets of paper. "This one here. It could be Sappho Rueb. The long silver hair with the asymmetrical cut. The jumper with a million pockets and everything falling out of them. Those old worn knee-high boots with the buckle on the ankle. And the face ... I can't get over how you gave her that hardened look while still making her vulnerable. Is that who you modeled it after?"

He nodded. "Can you pick out any others?"

She pointed at the large man with the bald head and scar across his cheek. "Vared Dubrok, for sure, and oh my gosh, this is an Isilki. Wow, it's like you got in the author's head." Her head. How had he managed to sketch these exactly as she'd envisioned them?

Rifling through a few more pages, she tapped on one. "Look, this is definitely Alcaeus Station. The spires right here. The helopads for short term transports. Then, the mountains in the distance over here and the ocean next to the cliffs of Gandhari. You've even got the tiny cave that Vared lives in until he teams up with Sappho. How in the world did you do this?"

Wes shrugged one shoulder, causing her to realize he only wore a pair of sweatpants. Oh, that wouldn't do. She tore her gaze away to focus on the drawings again.

"Elgato is such a great writer and describes these people and places so vividly that it was easy to draw. I visualized everything in my head."

She was still astounded that he'd picked up on exactly what her vision was with that story. What else did he have here? Some of the drawings she recognized, but not all. Yet every single one of them was extraordinary.

"Is this a different story?" She indicated a series of pages that had been collated together. At his nod, the gears in her mind started turning. And turning. "You should make these into a graphic novel. They're wonderful."

"I'd love to. If I had someone like Tempus Elgato writing the story, maybe I could make it a success. Right now, it's only some sketches. No real plot worked out yet."

Her eyes roamed the pages, and the gears in her head screeched to life. She picked up a drawing of a young woman on a dragon.

"I could totally see this playing out. Here, Teah Drach, the last of the dragon masters from the planet Alvaree, has gone on a quest to find a mate for her Chakrabati dragon, Rolla. She is the last of her kind and without a mate, the Chakrabati will die out. She can't let that happen because the Chakrabati have a substance in their saliva that heals. Her people have been using it for millennia to keep them alive and robust, something that is essential in fighting their bitter enemy, the Kallai."

One side of Wes' mouth lifted. "You got all that from these drawings?"

"Sure, look. This is Teah, and a full picture of her dragon is right here." She shuffled the pages to show him, then dug out another. "These are the Kallai warriors. All they know how to do is kill and collect the armor of their enemies as trophies. They are soulless creatures who thrill with the death of each victim. See how they have nothing behind their eyes? No remorse or feelings at all. It's as if they were created for one purpose only."

An idea formed. Scanning the pages on the table, she scooped another one up and swung to face him. "Yes, they were created for the purpose of killing, but not the people of Alvaree. That was a mistake. This is Corbet Murakam. He's responsible for the Kallai. He created them to help his people destroy the dark creatures that hunted and feasted on his tribe on the planet Sarvika. Somehow, they mutated and became the feared Kallai and traveled to the next planet, Alvaree."

She skimmed over the pages again and chose another one. "He teams up with Teah to get rid of the Kallai, for he is the only one who knows the secret computer code to stop them. However, he's never been able to get close enough before. With the help of her dragon, Rolla, they might be able to do it. They only need to get to the lead Kallai to cut the switch, but unfortunately, he is heavily guarded. She has to risk the life of her dragon to do this. With Rolla being the last of her kind, Teah is reluctant to put her in the way of danger. Corbet says if she helps, the Kallai will be gone, and he'll help her find a mate for Rolla."

She found another picture with two older, wizened characters. "They enlist the help of her grandmother, Zillah Sing, and his old tutor, Arion Toone, to help them come up with the plan."

As she rambled on with a story idea, Wes tilted his head and gazed at her strangely.

"What? It's too out there? You hate the story?"

He shuffled closer and tapped the pages she'd been waving about. "No, I love the idea. It's fascinating. Far better than anything I could have come up with."

"But you already came up with them. You drew these."

"They're simply drawings of people, places, and creatures. I didn't have a story in mind when I drew them. Not anything as interesting as what you came up with. You're very good in spinning tales. Have you ever thought of writing fantasy and adventure stories?"

"With my father?" Could she trust him with her secret? She was dying to tell someone who actually loved her work. Her friends supported her but weren't that into fantasy and adventure. *Here goes nothing.* "I'd have to get a pen name. Something like ... Tempus Elgato."

There. It was out in the world. Would he understand what she was saying?

"That one's already taken. You said you know the—" His eyes narrowed. "Wait. Are you telling me what I think you're telling me?"

Her face heated up to about a million degrees. Should she deny it or finally take the credit?

With hands planted on his hips, Wes examined her up and down. "No, way. It can't be ... because, if so, I'd have to fangirl really hard at your feet."

"Fangirl?"

He shrugged. "Sounds better than fanboy."

"No, you're my farm boy."

Chapter Eighteen

*H*e was staring at her as if she had three heads. He knew he was. But Tempus Elgato? He'd been reading these stories for a few years now and had always thought them brilliant. To realize the woman he'd been enamored with for the past two years was the writer he adored was too much. His head hurt.

It could also be the concussion he'd suffered yesterday.

"Are you okay, Wes?" Her soft voice grew concerned, and she entered his space, something he'd wanted her to do for a while but had never been successful at.

"Head's just a little achy. I should get something to eat. That might help."

She glanced at the table filled with sketches, then back at him. Did she want to keep on with the story she'd started creating? Or something else?

"Coffee's already made." She shrugged.

"You are an angel, for sure. Let me get my caffeine fix, then I want to know more about your secret identity."

He took her hand and led her to the kitchen. She didn't even tug it away. This was a definite improvement over her ignoring him for more than a year.

After pouring his coffee, he opened the fridge and glanced in. "What do you want for breakfast?"

Shaking her head, she steered him to the stool at the counter. "You've got a concussion, and I stayed here to make sure you don't overdo it. Sit. I'll whip something up."

As he sipped his coffee, he realized he hadn't added milk. Before he could get up, Tabitha appeared at his side and poured a splash of it into his mug.

"Definitely an angel. You don't need to wait on me. I'm not your father. I don't expect it."

Her faced stiffened, then relaxed. "You don't expect it, which is why I don't mind doing it. You've got bread and eggs. I can make French Toast."

"That would be yummy. I usually only get that when I go to the Willow Tree. Kayla always makes sure I get a little extra sprinkle of powdered sugar."

Tabitha frowned and glanced around. "Do you have powdered sugar here? If not, I can hardly sprinkle it on."

His frown followed hers. "No. I've only been here a short time and haven't really filled the pantry with all the necessities of life yet."

"You think powdered sugar is a necessity of life?" She chuckled, taking the eggs from the fridge and digging a large bowl from the cabinet.

"It is if I'm having French Toast," he said. "So how did you come about writing as Tempus Elgato? I've got to tell you, you've completely blown my mind. The part of it that wasn't scrambled yesterday from my fall."

"When I was in college, I took a few creative writing courses. Don't tell my dad. He doesn't know."

Wes put a finger to his lips and winked. "Our little secret. Along with the Russian spy lover and the pole dancing career."

A grin spread on her face, and she shook her head so the beautiful red hair swished around her shoulders. Man, he'd love to run his fingers through all that silk and see if it was as soft as it looked.

"Anyway, since I was binge-watching a bunch of sci-fi and fantasy, my mind, of course, came up with stories in that genre. My professor loved some of them and encouraged me to submit them to *Galaxia*, the magazine. He even gave me the contact information for the editor, who is a friend of his."

"Special treatment from the professor, huh?"

"I thought that at first, but he assured me it would just get me seen quicker. His friend has a reputation and would never publish something that wasn't the right quality. That made me feel better."

"So you published your first story while in college?"

"No, I was too chicken to send it back then. It wasn't until a few years later, when I was out of my mind bored with being the church secretary, that I finally decided to do it. I revised and edited the heck out of my best story and sent it in with a note, saying my professor had suggested it. It still took a month to hear back, but it was an offer."

"I'm glad you did, Tabitha. I can't tell you how much I enjoy your work. Still having a hard time wrapping my head around the fact you are my favorite author, sitting right here, cooking me breakfast."

Her face grew red, and she focused on the bread she was dipping in the egg mixture. Humble. He loved that about her. He wanted to keep her talking about this, keep her engaged in a conversation they both enjoyed.

"How long before you sent another story?"

The bread sizzled as she put it in the hot frying pan. "Publishing works slowly, and the story wasn't published for almost six months. Plus, I had to find a way to get the payment from them without my father knowing. I ended up renting a post office box in the next town over and having them send it there."

"Was it made out to Tempus Elgato?" he teased.

Her eyes widened. "I could hardly cash it if it was. I tolled long and hard coming up with the right name so no one would ever see it and tell my dad. When I told my friends what it was, Maggie figured it out right away."

He started running ideas through his mind. "Tempus means time. Elgato is cat in Spanish. Oh, wait, your father calls you Tabby Cat. I've heard him a few times."

"Sadly, you probably have. It's more than a little embarrassing at my age to have him do that in public. My last name, Dailey, is a measure of time."

He smirked. "That is incredibly clever. I'm even more bowled over at your creativity."

She flipped the French Toast onto two plates and brought it to the table. "Well, there isn't much creativity here with no powdered sugar to sprinkle on. I didn't even ask if you had syrup."

"I do." He quickstepped to the pantry and produced a bottle. "Only because I have frozen waffles in the freezer."

Her head tipped, her lips pulling to one side. "You had frozen waffles, and you still made me go through all this trouble."

He placed the syrup on the table along with a butter dish, then opened the fridge. "Sorry, but this is way better than frozen waffles. Do you want anything to drink other than your coffee? I usually like a glass of milk with mine."

"Milk would be great, thanks."

He brought both glasses to the table and sat next to her as she squeezed the syrup onto the plate. He followed suit, and they ate in silence for a few minutes, enjoying the homemade food.

Once he'd eaten half, he angled his head and asked, "So this story you started with my drawings. If Corbet—what was his name? We need to write these down, so we don't forget."

As he grabbed a pad of paper and pencil from the counter, she gazed up in thought.

"Um ... Murakam."

He scribbled it down, then glanced up. "How do you come up with these names so fast? You whipped them out like they were right there."

She shrugged and bit into another piece of toast. After chewing, she said, "I don't know. They just kind of come to me. A few of those were names I'd considered previously for stories that are hidden deeply away. You can find a random name generator online, and some of the names are strange but perfect for fantasy and science fiction. I also took Latin in high school, so I'll often use Latin words as roots for names and places."

"Fascinating." He scribbled down a few more details that he could remember of what she'd said earlier.

"So, what were you going to say about Corbet?" Her tone was almost reserved, like she didn't want to bring the attention back to her but kind of still did. So precious.

"I was thinking, if he created the Kallai warriors and they've been an enemy of her people for a long time, how old is he?"

Her face scrunched up making her appear much younger. "Oh, that's a plot hole. We can work it out, though. See, that's why two heads are better than one. I've never had anyone to bounce ideas off to get feedback."

"None of your friends have helped you?"

"They're super proud of my writing, but none of them actually read the genre. Maggie buries herself in farming books, Kayla prefers romance, and Aubrey loves the murder mysteries and grizzly thrillers. No one else knows I'm a science fiction author."

"Except me." He couldn't keep the grin from splitting his face. "I promise I won't say a word to anyone. Not unless you give me permission."

Her eyes widened. "Which I never will. All right, maybe years from now after my father passes away, but not until then."

He hated that she couldn't take credit for her incredible talent. On the other hand, he kind of liked that she assumed they'd still be friends long into the future. That's how he interpreted it, anyway.

"Are you heading into work today?"

She finished off her last piece of toast and shook her head. "I've had everything finished since Wednesday, and with Mrs. Chavez there, I don't have to worry. She told me to stay by your side and make sure you were okay."

An idea formed in his head. "I know I'm not supposed to be on any kind of screen for the next few days, but you can, and you're at my disposal today, sort of. Would you be interested in working on this story about Teah and Corbet and the Kallai warriors? I'd love to flesh it out and really get a full plot established."

Her eyes flashed with excitement. "I'd be very interested."

Chapter Nineteen

*E*nergy bubbled over inside Tabitha as she waited for the congregation to get their food at the potluck. Her friends sauntered over, having waited to get theirs with her. Too many ears once they sat at the tables.

"Miss Dailey appears to be brimming with sunshine today," Maggie pointed out.

"I noticed that, too. Could it be the shaggy-haired boy sitting next to her yet again in church today?" Aubrey lowered her sunglasses to her nose.

Kayla grinned. "That shaggy-haired boy also seems to be brimming with happiness today. Anything you wish to confess to us, Miss Dailey?"

Tabitha's eyes roamed the area, making sure all the eavesdroppers had finished filling their plates. She began her move down the table, taking her time choosing the right main meals and side dishes. Maggie sidled up behind her. Meanwhile, Aubrey and Kayla positioned themselves on the other side with their plates.

Aubrey threw her a look. "Spill girl, or it's going to burst out of you and make a terrible mess. Big Mama won't like that."

The woman in question clapped her hands and announced it was time to eat. Since Tabitha and her friends had a habit of lollygagging at the serving table, she didn't bother waiting for them. Which was good, because Tabitha had stuff to spill to her friends that couldn't be said with the others around.

"Wes had a little accident Thursday and got a slight concussion."

Kayla's face grew concerned. "That's not the reason you're so excited."

Maggie sighed. "She's building up to it like all good writers do. Give her time."

Tabitha peeked around again. "He needed someone to stay with him for at least forty-eight hours to make sure he was okay. He doesn't have any family around here."

Aubrey pursed her mulberry lips. "So, you volunteered. How interesting. What did Daddy have to say?"

Guilt heated her cheeks. "My father was at a conference until late yesterday afternoon."

Her three friends all gasped softly, their faces amused.

Kayla tossed a biscuit on her plate, then handed some to the others. "I thought you didn't like Wesley. In that way."

Tabitha rolled her eyes. "I don't. I was just there to help him if he needed it. I stayed in the extra bedroom upstairs, and he was in the master downstairs. Perfectly respectable."

"Then, why do you look like you've won the lottery?" Maggie scooped some of Cissy Hansen's ravioli onto her plate.

"I discovered something out of this world."

All three women froze and stared at her.

"He's really superman?" Aubrey's eyes twinkled.

Kayla grinned. "He's actually visiting royalty from a small country in Europe and is next in line to get the throne?"

Maggie groaned. "Kayla, you've been reading too many romance novels. Tell us, Tab, what is so exciting about the man you haven't wanted anything to do with for two years?"

"He draws pictures of space things. Fantasy creatures and aliens and futuristic cities. They are unbelievable!"

Aubrey pushed her glasses on the top of her head. "Just up your alley. Did you tell him what you do?"

"He already knows who Tempus Elgato is. He gets *Galaxia* magazine and loves the stories. We've been chatting about them at lunch." She wouldn't tell them it'd been several weeks of chatting and sharing.

"So he's a fan. Nice." Kayla sectioned off a piece of her mother's pecan pie and slapped it on her plate.

"And I told him it was me. He got all weird when he found out." She relayed how she'd found his drawings and then started creating a story out of thin air, which resulted in giving up her secret to him.

"So, you two have lots in common," Maggie said. "That's excellent."

Tabitha glanced down to see that Mrs. Mancini's rhubarb pie was already gone, like usual. But even that couldn't dim her mood. "That's not the best part. He loved the story I created and insisted we plan it out. We spent the better part of Friday and a little Saturday morning ironing out details and plot points. He even started sketching some of the secondary characters. This week he said we should get together and do a storyboard for each page. It'll be a graphic novel with him doing the pictures and me putting together the text."

Kayla tipped her head. "A graphic novel? Like a comic book?"

"Kind of, but way more detailed. And it's not a skimpy magazine size but an actual printed book."

"That is way cool, Tab." Aubrey winked.

Tabitha glanced around and realized some of the congregation had almost finished eating while they'd been standing here gabbing. Quickly, they took their plates and congregated around Donovan and Wesley who'd been having a heated conversation about some sports team.

"There's my wife." Donovan scooted over to make room for Maggie. "I thought you'd deserted me already after only a month of wedded bliss."

Tabitha took a place next to Wesley, and his face beamed. It was rare she chose to sit near him. Usually, it was forced upon her or manipulated by the others. After the connection they'd made with the story, her tune had started to change.

Kayla and Aubrey flanked the group, and they all attacked the now lukewarm food. It didn't matter. Tabitha had never felt such a high before. Even when she'd gotten her first story published, it hadn't felt this good because she hadn't dared tell anyone. Now, not only did her best friends know, but Wesley was right in there with her creating alongside her. It was invigorating.

"How's the head, Wes?" Kayla asked in between bites.

"It's better. I have to keep from shaking it too much, though, or I get a bongo solo. Stupid accident. I wasn't paying as much attention as I should have been."

Aubrey snickered. "Now, what could possibly have taken your mind off your work? Maggie, didn't you say Wesley was typically a very cautious worker?"

Maggie grinned and slanted a glance at her husband. "Yes, very. Must be the church environment. Must figure God will take care of him because he's fixing up the church."

"Tabitha," Kayla purred. "You'll need to make sure Wesley doesn't get distracted while he's on a ladder next time. We'd hate to see him hurt again."

Wes peered around, and Tabitha could tell he was a bit confused. She patted his hand. "Don't pay any attention to these women. They're all completely ridiculous."

"If you say so. They're your friends." He finished his chicken casserole and started in on his piece of Mrs. Mancini's rhubarb pie.

"Oh," Tabitha mused. "I wish I could be first in line someday to finally try some of Mrs. Mancini's pies. Everyone says they're the best."

Wes scowled. His fork stilled on the way to his mouth. "You've never gotten to try this?"

"It's always gone by the time I get there." Tabitha shrugged and worked on her sweet and sour kielbasa.

Donovan cleared his throat. "Maybe if your friends got in line earlier and didn't wait around kibitzing forever, they could save you a piece."

"We could do that, Tab," Aubrey suggested. "Next week. I promise to shove everyone aside and get you a piece."

Kayla laughed. "I bet you could get her a piece without shoving people aside, too. Aubrey."

Aubrey rolled her eyes. "Where's the fun in that?"

Wesley nudged his plate closer to Tabitha and whispered, "You can have my piece if you want. I already took a tiny bite, but if you don't mind that, you're welcome to the rest."

Something warm and fuzzy filled her at the gentle offer. He was getting too close. She had to push him away and back off. But then they couldn't do the collaboration. She hadn't ever been so excited for something in her life. Was it time to compromise some of her life goals while still reaching others?

She stuck her fork in the pie on his plate and scooped up a bite. "Thank you. But I really think we should share it."

Chapter Twenty

*T*he summer sun shone brightly, and Wes could tell it would be an idyllic day. Tabitha had agreed to go tubing down the New River with him. Mostly so they could discuss the graphic novel they'd been working on and still have fun outside.

He'd worked almost every night, creating new sketches and learning the ins and outs of exactly what was involved in getting a graphic novel published. They could go the traditional route and submit to a publishing house. Unfortunately, many of them required you to have an agent. Getting an agent seemed even harder than getting a book published. Then, he'd read that some publishers didn't want an author to have their own illustrator and typically wanted to use in-house staff.

Another option was to self-publish, but there were so many things to learn it seemed it would take them forever to figure it out.

A third option was a vanity press, but he'd been warned away from those because they usually charged you tons of money and insisted you buy a hefty number of books before they published.

He had an e-mail into an old college friend who knew people in the publishing business asking for some advice. Hopefully, he'd hear back soon.

Tabitha pulled into his driveway right on time, and he ran out to meet her. His SUV was already loaded with the inner tubes, towels, and his floating cooler was filled with snacks.

"Do you already have your bathing suit on?"

She nodded and pulled aside her top to reveal a dark blue strap. He wondered if she was a bikini type of gal, but then her father would probably never let her out of the house with something like that on.

"We'll keep your car here and take mine to the starting point. With how slow the river is at this time of year, it should take us a few hours to finally reach my house."

Tabitha grinned. "You'll have to make sure you pay attention, so we don't float on past."

He flicked his thumb over his shoulder. "I put a couple of bright yellow plastic chairs near the water and stuck a small floating dock on shore. Hopefully, we don't miss those."

"Hopefully." Her smile was infectious.

The drive was fun with them reviewing what they'd already plotted and devised for the graphic novel. Wes had more sketches to show Tabitha, but he'd wait until they got back to the house. He was hoping to convince her to stay for dinner as well. He had food for the grill and had made some side dishes. If she didn't stay, he could bring them to the potluck tomorrow at church.

There were already plenty of vehicles at the drop off location, but he was able to find a place to park and unload the SUV.

"Do you want to put your cover up in the car so it doesn't get wet or were you planning to bring it along?"

Her lips thinned, and she glanced around. He didn't recognize anyone as this spot was popular for miles around. Her shoulders eventually relaxed.

"I'll leave it here. I just didn't want any of Dad's congregation to see me out and about in only a bathing suit."

"You're allowed to have fun like any other person, Tabitha. Even though I wouldn't mind seeing you in a skimpy suit, for some reason, I doubt your bathing attire is scandalous." He winked and she laughed, then reached for the bottom of her long, over-sized shirt.

Sure enough, the suit had boy shorts and a top cut like a tank top. It definitely showed more of her figure than she ever had with him around, but usually her wardrobe was ultra conservative or kind of baggy.

They retrieved the tubes, the floating cooler, and a waterproof bag he'd stuffed towels and his phone in. After locking his SUV, they hauled the stuff to the edge of the water, and he attached the cooler to his tube.

"Do you want to be attached, as well, or are you more of the free-floating kind of tuber?"

Her lips quirked up on one side. "I haven't done this a ton and certainly not in recent years. Usually, it was with either Maggie or Kayla's family. Then, we wanted to be away from the parentals and Kayla's annoying brothers."

"So, I'll keep you unattached."

"Actually ..." She tipped her head, her gaze bouncing between the tubes and the cooler. "You brought drinks and snacks, right?"

"Bottles of water, soda, and tea, along with snacks and a few sandwiches."

"Then, I guess I'd like to be attached. I don't want you taking all the food. This way I get equal access."

He grinned at her, secretly thrilled. "I'd never take all the food, but it isn't always easy to make your way in the current to the cooler."

He clipped the cooler in between the tubes and dragged them into the water. Tabitha stuck her toes in, and happiness radiated off her face. He'd been able to do that for her. God willing, she'd let him do it more often.

Once in the water, the current slowly swirled them downstream. The water level was low this time of year, and a few times they scraped the bottom. Wes had to push them back into the stream of flowing river.

They chatted about some of the locals, and Tabitha mentioned a couple who had lost their home recently.

"My father's been rallying folks to help them out. It was horrible. They only missed two mortgage payments. Mr. Handler had finally gotten a new job and scraped up enough to pay off the two months with the late payment fees. The bank manager wouldn't even allow it. He foreclosed on the property, and they've lost everything. That house was all the equity they had."

Wes had heard of unethical bankers who had no sympathy for anyone's troubles. It reminded him too much of one he knew well.

"This was a banker here in town?" There were only two banks in Prescott Hill, and Mr. Prescott, Big Mama's husband, owned one. He may be high and mighty, but he was usually amicable and willing to work with those who truly were under duress.

"No, unfortunately, they went to a bank in Roanoke since Mrs. Handler's family is from there. It was a bad decision, though when they made it twelve years ago, they didn't realize it."

"One reason I left the city. Too impersonal. It's every man for himself there, not neighbor helping neighbor."

"Yeah, well, this Arthur Lipton certainly wasn't very neighborly."

Wesley's lungs dried up. "Arthur Lipton is the banker?" He didn't really need the answer. He already knew.

"Yes. I feel so bad for the Handlers. Now, the bank will take the house and most everything in it to sell and pay the loan."

Pulling a soda from the cooler, Wes thought about the Handler family. Nice couple with two young children. Paul was a good, hard worker. They shouldn't have their house taken away like that. Not after putting in twelve years' worth of payments. To his grandfather of all people.

His mind whirled with thoughts of some way he could help fix the situation. Could he talk to his grandfather and convince him to give the family another shot, especially since they now had the back payments and Paul had another job? Possibly, but for sure, he'd want something from Wes. Nothing came free from that man.

"I've got quite a bit of money saved," Tabitha broke into his thoughts. "I wondered about giving it to them to help them out, but it sounds like the bank foreclosure is a done deal."

Wes didn't want Tabitha within fifty miles of Arthur Lipton, certainly not asking him for a favor. No chance he'd do it for some little church secretary from the hills of Virginia, anyway. His grandfather didn't have a warm or caring bone in his body, unlike Tim Roberts, the grandfather who had spent so much time teaching him to build with his hands, giving him a purpose and pride in a job done well.

Wes still had friends in the banking industry back in Roanoke. He also had a sizeable chunk of cash with which to purchase a foreclosed house. Yeah, he'd have to get on the phone to a few people tonight after Tabitha left. A shame, because he didn't want her to leave. He'd love for her to stay forever. Wouldn't happen. Definitely not today.

After taking a handful of chips and chomping on them, he asked, "What did you have planned for all that money you saved up? Something fun or frivolous?"

She laughed. "My father would have a cow if I bought something frivolous. You should have heard him go on about the hat you bought me before I hinted Maggie had given it to me."

"I don't get credit for that, huh?"

She reached out and took his hand across the cooler and kept it there. "You get credit from me. That's all that matters. Not to mention, my friends all know you bought it. I'm sure Maggie mentioned it to Donovan, too."

"So, if nothing frivolous, what then?"

Her cheeks heated and not from the bright sun overhead. He loved seeing her pale skin blush. "I've saved almost enough for six months of rent in Roanoke."

"You plan to rent an apartment in Roanoke? Does your father know this?"

"No, not yet. I've still got more planning and research to do. I've got to find a job that pays enough for me to live on, and I want at least six months back up just in case."

"You don't want to stay in town?"

She tipped her head. "I told you this. It's why I always pushed away your advances."

"Not recently. We've hung out a lot lately." Not that they'd done anything even remotely romantic, but it was still time together.

"Yes, because of the science fiction stories. The ones from the magazine and now the one we're co-writing." Her eyes scanned the area like she thought a spy would jump up and capture her words to take back to her father.

"You only like me for my geekiness."

She rolled her eyes. "Your geekiness and artistic talent. Plus, you're kind of fun to hang around."

The last words had him singing the Hallelujah chorus.

"What kind of work would you look for in the city?" He hated the thought of her wandering the crowded streets. She wasn't completely naive, but she wasn't exactly street smart either.

"I don't know. I've done all sorts of office work, some accounting and transcription. It's a good-sized city. There should be something that will pay well enough to live there."

"I lived in Roanoke, and the jobs definitely pay more than here in Prescott Hill, but the rents are much higher, too. There are some areas of town that are more affordable. They aren't what I'd call safe for a young lady, though. I'd worry about you there." He'd miss her, too. Might have to go after her and save her from herself. Swoop to the rescue like an action-adventure character. Would she consider him more if he lived in the city with her? Could he give up this beautiful life in the New River Valley to stay with her in the city he hated?

Maybe. Maybe he could do it for a short time, then convince her to return. After she'd had her fun and adventure.

"Oh, hey." Her head whipped toward him, the soft breezing tugging on a few strands of red hair. "I thought of a way to get rid of that plot hole regarding Teah and where she got her dragon."

"Great. What'd you come up with?"

They chatted about the story for a while and, between the two of them, scraped up enough details to fix the inconsistency they'd created. She had such an incredible imagination. It would be a waste if she couldn't do more with it on a full-time basis. He'd love to offer her the opportunity to write all the time and not worry about finances. At the same time, he needed her to want to be with him for him. Tabitha could never be a gold digger—she didn't have it in her—but there had to be some deep feelings on her part before he'd put himself in that kind of predicament.

"I want to eventually put all my short magazine stories together and weave them into this epic fantasy adventure. You noticed how many of them interconnected. I've already got tons of notes on what to add to mesh them into one humongous novel. Maybe even a series."

"You are amazing, you know that? Are you allowed to do something like that with them? What does your contract with the magazine say about it?"

"I can use the stories any way I want after they've been out in the wild for at least six months."

He thought back to when her last one had come out. Just a month ago. "How many more stories have you contracted to write for them?"

"They only offer for stories once they've been written. Though I have to say I pretty much get a yes within hours of sending one in now. I've only got one in with them at this point, but there are two more ready to go. I haven't sent those in yet. I want to clean them up a bit first."

"Maybe you should wait. Let the others run out past the six-month mark. By then, we could be closer to finishing the graphic novel. I'm still doing research on the best way to publish it. A friend of mine said if you've already got a ready-made audience, it'll be easier. Once you get your rights to them back, you can start weaving them together like you want."

Her eyes stared into his. "I do want."

If only she was talking about him.

Chapter Twenty-One

*W*es was giving her ideas she'd only dreamed of. Okay, she'd imagined some of them but honestly hadn't thought they'd ever come to fruition. Working together on the graphic novel had finally given her a flicker of hope that perhaps she could do this, be even a little bit successful with her writing.

Oh, they probably wouldn't sell millions of copies of the book, but even if they just got it out there and sold some, she'd be happy. The magazine said the issues with her stories always sold out. That had to mean something.

Today, floating lazily down the river, had been the most fun she'd had in the longest time. Usually, fun came in the shape of Maggie, Aubrey, and Kayla. Today, it looked like a shaggy puppy in aviator sunglasses and the nicest chest she'd seen. Unless you counted online or the covers of Kayla's romance novels, she hadn't had many chances to gaze at a variety of male chests, but Wesley's was one that made her salivate. He was muscular in a lean sort of way and had just the right amount of chest hair. A sprinkle here and there. Nothing too much. They'd been floating for almost two hours now, and it was hard to look away.

The sight of two bright yellow chairs on the shore shook her out of her happy stupor. They'd come to the end of the line. For floating, anyway. If she got him talking about their collaboration, could she hang out longer? Most likely. Wes had been nothing but a gentleman whenever she came over, but Tabitha knew he wanted her there. Tabitha, the woman, not Tempus Elgato, the writer. He'd been making plays for her for over a year.

She pointed to the yellow chairs. "Looks like we made it, just in time. The cooler's getting empty."

They'd stopped on a few sand bars and eaten the sandwiches he'd brought. She'd never even thought to offer to bring something. Her father might have gotten the impression she was going to the used book store to find some good books to add to the church bookshelves. Taking a basket of food along would have been hard to explain.

Wes slipped out of his tube and dragged both tubes and the attached cooler over to shore. Once he stopped, she popped out and waded the rest of the way. The river had been so refreshing today, she almost hated to get out. Good thing she'd put on plenty of sunblock.

With the tubes on shore, Wes disconnected them and dragged them up the hill to shove under his back deck. Tabitha retrieved the towel from her bag and dried off her legs and suit, then wrapped it around her waist. She'd been exposed to his eyes all day, but now that she wasn't sitting in the tube, she felt self-conscious.

Wes jogged back to her and motioned to the chairs. "Do you want to sit here for a bit or head up the house?"

"As much as I'd ordinarily love to sit by the river, we've been floating in it all day, and I need to stand for a bit. I should probably put some aloe on my skin, so it doesn't dry up too much."

"I agree. Want to grab the other side of the cooler so we can get it up the hill?"

They got the rest of the gear up to his back deck, then she skipped to her car to retrieve the bag of extra clothes she'd brought.

Wes excused himself to take a quick shower and offered her the use of one of the other two. She did a perfunctory wipe down with a facecloth, lotioned up, then donned a cute sundress that wouldn't rub anywhere if she'd gotten too much sun.

When she returned to the sunken living room, Wes stood at the windows, gazing out at the river they'd spent an amazing time on.

Touching his arm, she smiled at him. "Thanks for taking me out today. It was a blast and so incredibly relaxing. I can't remember the last time I just floated around doing nothing."

"Doing nothing?" He made a face and planted his hands on his hips. "We did some major revision work on our novel. All we have to do now is listen to the tape and get it written down."

"I can't believe you brought a waterproof recorder. It was perfect. Better than trying to use paper in the river."

"I have my moments." His smile reached his eyes, and she wanted to touch his lips to capture that happiness.

"Yes, you do. Should I drive you back now to get your car?"

He shook his head. "No, I don't want to sit again for that long. We'll get it later, unless you're in a hurry to leave. I wasn't sure if you had plans for later."

"No plans for a while." Like the entire night, not that she'd stay here overnight. He didn't have a concussion any longer.

"Good. I was hoping to talk you into sharing the steaks I marinated earlier. I can't possibly eat both of them. I've also got side dishes to go along with them."

"What if I said no?" She was being sassy. She'd love to spend more time with him. What a change from a few months ago, huh?

"Then, I'd cook up both steaks, use one for a stew later, and bring all the side dishes to the potluck tomorrow. I'd much rather share it with you."

"I think I could be talked into staying. My father will be working on last minute changes to tomorrow's sermon. He hates to be interrupted. Probably won't even notice I'm gone."

"I'd notice." Wes took one of her hands and stroked the skin on the back of it. "Thanks for coming with me today. I had a great time, too."

"I was wondering … I'd love to see your interpretation of some of my other characters. If I do this epic fantasy adventure with all my short stories hooked together, it might be cool to have a few pictures in it. Nothing like the graphic novel, but I was thinking of something on each chapter heading or just a quick sketch to show what the characters look like."

"I'd be honored. I already have many of them done. Were there any characters you specifically had in mind?"

He took her elbow and steered her down the hallway to his office. They hovered over his desk and shuffled through the papers already there. After making a quick notation of what she wanted, he studied her. What exactly did he see?

"I'll assume you don't have a website for Tempus."

She shook her head. "I've never really thought of doing that. Mostly because I didn't want anything tracing Elgato back to me. It's not like I can go do Comic Con or anything like that."

"There are ways of keeping your identity a secret. First, you need to set up an e-mail account in Tempus Elgato's name."

"You can do that?"

"You can set up multiple accounts. I'd actually have you do one for business, like talking to editors or ordering supplies. Then, you'll need one for fans. That should be separate."

She laughed at his outrageous suggestion. "Like I have so many of those."

He tapped her on the nose. "You've got me. Long before I knew Tempus was Miss Tabitha Dailey, daughter of the good reverend. I imagine I'm not the only one who's enamored with your writing. *Galaxia* has a huge following. I can help you set up a website. I did some web design in my last job and would be happy to get you started. You need an online presence."

Her grin wrinkled her nose. "Well, if you're going to be doing a book with the famous Tempus Elgato, then maybe you should have a website for your pictures, too."

His lips curled, and his eyes gleamed. "Maybe I should. But do I use my real name? That might link you back to me. I think it's a shame you can't take the credit right now for your work, though I understand why. I wouldn't want to cause you any problems."

"Do you have a pen name in mind?"

"Something out there like Tempus?"

She bumped her shoulder into his. "Hey, that one's taken. Find your own. You could do something simple like Art Sketch."

He narrowed his eyes at her and laughed. "I hope you aren't serious."

"We'll give it some thought. We don't have to choose one right now."

His eyebrows waggled up and down. "I should have some sort of a pirate name."

Wesley said a little prayer for forgiveness and tapped on Reverend Dailey's office door. The man glanced up and smiled.

"What can I do for you, Mr. Roberts? Is there a problem with the addition?"

"No, sir. Ahead of schedule still. I'm getting close to needing some of the hardware for the doors, cabinets, and windows. I know you're far too busy to pick these out, but I want to make sure I get something that will be acceptable to the church."

"Hmm. Yes, I see. Can Tabitha help you with this? It's Thursday, and with Mrs. Chavez being here, I imagine she's ahead of her schedule as well. I can let her loose for tomorrow if that works."

"It does. However, there isn't a lot of choice here in town for what I need. I've got some business in Roanoke tomorrow—you know my family is from there—and I thought Tabitha could come into the city for a few days. Her friend, Maggie, plans to stay with Donovan at his grandparents' house tomorrow and Saturday. I imagine she'd be welcome to stay with them."

Had he given the man the impression that he'd be staying with his family? Like that would happen. If they pulled this off, he'd be staying at Donovan's grandparents' house, too. Donovan's grandparents were currently in Europe on vacation and had let their grandson know he could use their residence anytime he wanted. Apparently, the place had a multitude of spare bedrooms, so he and Tabitha could both stay there. Not in the same room, but close by. He had some plans for her.

"Oh, I think that would work. Tabitha hasn't been into the city much in the past few years, so you'll need to pick her up and bring her to the hardware stores."

"I'm happy to cart her around, especially since she'll be helping me find the perfect details to finish up this addition."

"Excellent. Now that that's settled, excuse me while I get back to my sermon. These parishioners expect heavenly guidance every Sunday when they get here. I have to make it perfect."

"Thank you, sir. I'll let Tabitha know the plans."

As he walked out of the reverend's office and closed the door, Tabitha sidled next to him. "Did it work?"

"You're all set to stay with Maggie and Donovan at his grandparents' place in Roanoke."

Her eyes narrowed. "And what about you?"

"I mentioned I have family in the city."

Her eyes gleamed. "Did you mention you weren't actually staying with them?"

His head tilted to the side. "That may have slipped my mind. Your father's a busy man and needed to get back to his sermon. The congregation is counting on him for heavenly guidance."

"Thank heaven for that guidance." He loved when her face glowed.

"Have you finished your work for the week? Your father figured you might have."

Tabitha's lips twitched. "Mrs. Chavez has been a godsend."

"So, you have time to meet in the conference room and go through some websites for hardware?" He indicated the room next to her office.

"I thought we were doing that tomorrow."

"We'll be purchasing the hardware tomorrow. It would be prudent to go through the hundreds of different kinds today and narrow it down."

"Narrow it down. Good idea."

"Otherwise, we'd spend all day at a dozen different places comparing, then have to run back to earlier stores because that would be where the ones we wanted were."

Tabitha grinned. "Of course we would. This saves us time. Then, whatever will we do with the rest of the day?"

Wes attempted to keep his expression neutral. He couldn't tell her there was a science fiction convention in the city this weekend. Doubtful she could hide her excitement if he said they were going. Plus, he wanted it to be a surprise. Maggie and Donovan knew. It was why they'd offered to head into the city, as well. Camouflage.

"There's lots to see in Roanoke. I'm sure we'll find something. Let's get cracking on the fixtures. I've got a bunch of places bookmarked on my iPad."

"Let me just tell Mrs. Chavez where we'll be and grab that list of materials you gave us a few weeks ago. I can check them off as we decide."

Wes straggled into the conference room with his computer and arranged two chairs side by side at the table. Tabitha joined him with a pile of papers a few minutes later and shut the door behind her.

As she settled next to him, she giggled. "Aubrey was brilliant to suggest getting that woman to volunteer here. She can run everything in the office now and is so personable on the phone. I have nothing left to teach her."

"Gives you time to do stuff like this." He patted her hand, and a thrill raced through him as she stared at their hands and a tiny smile touched her lips. Progress.

He booted up the iPad and started scrolling through the sites he'd bookmarked. "Get that list out and let's see if we can narrow down the characteristics of these pieces."

They spent the next few hours scrolling through sites and taking notes. He loved that she stayed close to him as they peered at the screen together comparing products and prices.

"Oh, I should let Maggie know we're all set for tomorrow." Tabitha gazed up from the screen. "Are we driving in with them?"

Wes lifted one shoulder. "I'll need my car since we'll be going in different directions from Maggie and Donovan. Can you be ready to leave early? I want to get in and out with this hardware."

"Depends what you mean by early. I'm usually at my desk by eight, but I can be ready before that."

"Let's try for seven-thirty. Is Mrs. Chavez all set to man the church office tomorrow?"

Tabitha nodded. "Yes, she's happy to be kept busy. It would be great if she can get my father to actually have lunch outside again like she did last week. That was unexpected."

"Your father seems to get a little flustered around her, I noticed."

Tabitha's eyes narrowed. "He does, and I find that very interesting. No one has ever flustered him. Not that I recall."

"It's been years since your mom passed away. Has he dated since then?"

"Never. Not that I would have minded. Is that what you think it is? He has a crush on Mrs. Chavez?"

Wes shrugged. "Lots of guys get nervous in the presence of a beautiful lady. Mrs. Chavez is certainly quite charming and lovely."

Her eyes gleamed. "Maybe we ought to try and leave them alone together more often."

Wes moved so his shoulder touched hers. "You might suggest to Mrs. Chavez that your father is here to help her if she has any questions."

Her head dropped to his arm. "If what you're suggesting is right, she may just find lots of questions to ask him, even if she doesn't really have any."

"Exactly."

Chapter Twenty-Two

*T*abitha chuckled as Wesley and Donovan both grabbed for the check. The restaurant they'd had lunch at, a fancy bistro in downtown Roanoke, had a great view of the city market and all the visitors bustling about to get fresh food for the week.

The air wasn't as fresh as Prescott Hill, but there was definitely a vibrancy surrounding them. Tabitha could see herself living here. For a short while. Long enough to convince her father she was capable of being on her own and succeeding.

The men both pulled out bills and threw them on the tray as the server passed by. If Tabitha's calculations were correct, the waitress would be one happy lady. When they told her they didn't need any change, her entire face beamed.

"What do we do now?" Tabitha gazed at her companions. "I can't believe it took so little time to get all that hardware for the church this morning."

Wes patted her hand, and she didn't pull it away. It was getting harder to do that as the days went by and their connection deepened on so many levels.

"That's because we did our research first. I even put in orders for most of the stuff so we wouldn't be disappointed when we got here."

"Smart of you, Mr. Roberts, but now we have all this time here in the big city. Maggie, did you two have something specific you wanted to do?"

"Donovan and I want to check out the farmer's market here to get ideas for Popham Farm. We might hit a museum later and possibly a show tonight."

Tabitha got the feeling her friend hadn't planned on including them in their itinerary. It was understandable. Maggie and Donovan hadn't been married all that long and needed some quality time together. They certainly didn't get much alone time at the farm with all the kids and the ranch hands.

Wes skimmed his hand up her back, causing tingles to bubble up through her limbs. "I've got some plans for us I think you'll enjoy. We can meet Donovan and Maggie back at his grandparents' house later."

They all gathered together, and as Tabitha hugged her friend goodbye, Maggie whispered, "Have fun."

"You know what we're doing?"

Maggie just smiled and trotted off with her husband. Wes hooked her elbow and steered her away from the restaurant, down the street.

"Are we getting the car at the parking garage first?" Where was he taking her? He'd been trying to hide a grin all morning, and she hadn't known why. Figured it was because they'd pulled a fast one over on her father. Perhaps not.

"It's only about a fifteen-minute walk from here. Since it's a nice day, I thought that would be okay. You indicated you wanted to see some of the city."

"That would be great. Thanks. Are you going to tell me where we're going, or are we just wandering around exploring? Because I'm okay with that, too."

"I have a destination in mind. Come on."

She linked her arm with his, and her head swiveled from side to side as they strolled through the city. At one point, there was a huge sign for the civic center, and she froze.

"There's a science fiction convention at the Berglund Center?" She tipped her head toward the sign.

"Are you interested in going?"

Was he serious? "Am I interested? Is the sky blue? Did you have this planned the whole time?"

His lips twitched. "Yeah. I mean, we had to get the hardware for the addition. Honestly, though, I won't be ready to install any of it for another few weeks. The trip could have waited, but the convention would be done by then."

Her heart constricted and she wanted to shout, "I love you." But did she? Love him? She'd been fighting it for months now. Years, actually. She'd let her guard down since he'd been doing the addition, and it seemed he'd slipped right in. She didn't know whether to laugh or cry.

Instead, she threw herself into his arms and hugged him. He curled his arms around her and held tight. "I'm going to take that to mean you approve."

After a last squeeze, she eased back. "Most definitely. I never even looked to see who's here."

He led her to the line that flowed toward the main doors. "Lots of people who were in shows and movies that have the word 'star' in them. You might have heard of a few."

They stopped to peruse the large banner on the wall inside the doors. She couldn't believe her eyes at the number of famous people—famous in the science fiction world, anyway—that were here. Some were only here for one day, but a few were here for both. A good number were here today.

"Oh, look at all these people. We need to get a brochure and find out if they have any panels or picture signings soon. I hope we haven't missed out."

Wes plucked a brochure from a nearby table as they queued toward the security doors. Tabitha didn't even pay attention as he paid for the tickets and only half noticed them asking to view inside her purse.

"I can't believe you brought me here. Even if I don't get to see any of these stars, it'll be better than anything I've ever done. I'm so excited." She couldn't stop the little bounce in her step and the quiver in her body.

Once they were inside the huge auditorium. Wes tugged her to the side, out of the way of traffic. "Let's peek at the schedule and plan out what you want to do. Walking through all the vendors can be done in between any of the panels or signings."

Tabitha wasn't sure she could concentrate on the brochure as anticipation thrummed through her. Wes draped one arm over her shoulder and pointed with the other.

"There's a panel with three of the *Stargate Atlantis* cast in about thirty minutes. Do you want to see that one?"

"Of course I do. It'll probably be sold out, though. Everyone will want to see them."

"The panels are all part of your ticket. If we head there now and wait in line, we should be able to get a spot."

"Yes, yes, yes. Please." Wes laughed, and she felt silly. "I'm sorry. I know I'm being ridiculous, but I can't believe I get to be here."

"You're not being ridiculous at all. I'm super stoked to be here, too. Let's go get in line."

He consulted the map, and they made their way through the large crowd, up an escalator, and down a long hallway. There was already a line outside the door, but Tabitha didn't think it was too bad. If the room the panel was in was good-sized, they would likely get a seat.

As people all around them buzzed with the same kind of energy, Tabitha began to realize she wasn't the only eager one here.

Wes held the brochure between them again and peered down. "Want to get a picture taken with John Sheppard and Ronon Dex?"

Tabitha stared at him. "You keep asking these ridiculous questions like I'm going to say no for some strange reason. Although," she glanced surreptitiously around, then back at him. "I kind of feel guilty, like I'm doing something wrong."

He scowled. "Why?"

She kept her voice soft. "My father thinks all this is a waste of time. He doesn't read fiction. Ever. If it doesn't tell you how to improve yourself or give you the details of the life of some godly man, he has no interest in it."

"He doesn't have to have an interest in it. Doesn't mean you can't. You have a right to enjoy stuff that he doesn't and vice versa. No one's right or wrong."

She bit her lip to keep from saying that wasn't how she was raised, but today was just too good a day. She'd had a great morning with Wes choosing the hardware for the church, had lunch with good friends at a lovely downtown location, and now she was with a very handsome, charming man who'd given her an opportunity she'd never have given to herself.

Suddenly, the line began to move, and she peeked to see the doors to the room open. Slowly, they made their way in, and Wes, being quite a bit taller than her, perused for empty seats. Catching her elbow, he hustled her up a few rows and pardoned them as they scurried to two empty seats right in the middle of the second row.

A large man sat in front of her, and she almost cried, but then he shifted down a few seats and a small child ended up in there. Tabitha had an unobstructed view of the stage.

Wesley glanced down at the face of the woman next to him and wanted nothing more than to kiss her beautiful lips. Her enthusiasm was contagious, but it was her absolute joy that wrapped him in its tendrils and yanked her closer to his heart. If he hadn't already known he was in love with her, he would now. He wished he could give her everything she ever wanted and always have her gaze at him like he'd hung the moon and stars.

Before he could say anything to her, the lights flickered and a voice came over the intercom, announcing the three cast members. Tabitha squeezed his hand so tight he thought he might lose circulation. Worth it.

She watched with rapt attention as each of the cast strolled onstage and greeted the audience. The emcee started by asking a question for each of them to answer, but soon the actors, who'd worked together for years, went off on tangents with anecdotes of when they were filming and some of the shenanigans that happened on set. The three stars were engaging and goofy and completely fun, and Tabitha's gaze never left the front of the room. A huge smile had permanently plastered itself to her face.

The banter and laughter never slowed down, until the announcer declared it was time to wrap things up. Tabitha kept her eyes on them until they'd wandered beyond the curtain in the back of the room. As people stood and began to leave, she whipped toward him and gasped.

"That was so incredible. If we don't do anything else, that was worth it."

Wes shrugged, his grin turning crooked. "So, you're good? You don't want to get a picture taken with two of them? Because I already bought the ticket." He held up his phone to show the QR code.

Grabbing his hand, she jumped up and down. "You arranged for a picture with them? When did you do this? I didn't think you were serious before."

"Did it while you were mesmerized. We can go get in the queue for pictures in about ten minutes. I have an idea, though. We have to make a quick stop."

Having Tabitha's hand on his arm wasn't something he'd ever complain about. She was practically in a trance as he guided her back through the hall, down the escalator, and into the large auditorium again.

When he purchased four plastic lightsabers, she frowned at him. "Lightsabers are from *Star Wars*. John Sheppard and Ronon Dex are from *Stargate*."

He smirked at her. "I'll bet they don't complain."

Sure enough, when it was their time to go behind the curtain with the cast members, and Wes handed the men their weapons, they all immediately took poses like they were having a four-way duel. The moment couldn't last too long as others had also paid to have photos with the stars, but they'd have a memento to take with them.

It was only a few minutes before their picture showed up on the table outside the booth. Tabitha's eyes sparkled with delight when she saw the pose. The actors had gotten into character, fierce expressions on their faces.

"Do you want to walk around the displays for a bit, or was there another panel you wanted to see?"

Tabitha sighed. "How about we wander around for a little while? I'm so keyed up I think I need to calm down."

She held the envelope with their photo lovingly against her chest and clutched his arm with her other hand. They pored over the merchandise as they passed table after table filled with mugs, figures, t-shirts, key chains, magnets, comic books, and every other thing one could imagine.

"Let me know if you want me to buy any of this for you."

"You've already done so much just bringing me here, I can't ask for any more. Not to mention, where would I put it? My father doesn't exactly know about this little field trip, and I doubt he'd approve."

"If there's anything you can't live without, you can always house it at my place. I won't even charge you a huge storage fee."

Her eyes narrowed, then she laughed. God, she was exquisite when she was happy. He wanted to keep her that way always. Something caught the corner of his eye, and he steered her toward a large corner booth.

When she saw where he was taking her, she halted. "*Galaxia* magazine. I didn't know they'd have a booth here."

"We should take a peek. I hear they have some talented authors who write for them."

"We have the most excellent authors working for us," one of the men called out after hearing his words. "Are you familiar with our magazine?"

"Oh, yes. We both read it all the time. Every issue." Tabitha bit her lip, and Wes wondered if she wanted to spill her little secret or keep it to herself.

Wes thumbed through the newest issue and paused at a page. "Do you have more stories from Tempus Elgato coming soon?"

The man nodded. "We've got two more contracted. After that, I'm not sure. I've been meaning to contact Elgato to see."

A couple in their late teens next to them whipped around. "Are those stories from Elgato coming out soon? Man, that writer sure can get you on the edge of your seat. I wish he'd write an entire book, so I don't have to wait so long in between issues."

"Oh, my God, a book by Tempus Elgato would be out of this world," the girlfriend screeched.

Tabitha remained still next to him, but she practically vibrated as these people discussed her.

"I may need to reach out and suggest that. I'm the point person with Elgato," the man in the booth said it like his connection with the author made him a hotshot.

"You're Rory Beecham?" Tabitha asked.

Rory tipped his head at her. "Yes, how do you know me?"

The deer in the headlights look on Tabitha's face was cute, but Wes figured she wasn't ready to spill the beans yet.

"Everyone knows Rory Beecham is the executive editor for Galaxia."

The man puffed up again, and Wes almost rolled his eyes. What would he do if he knew Tempus Elgato was standing in the flesh right next to him? Could be he'd associated with enough celebrities that he wouldn't be fazed.

The teen girl bounced closer to Rory and gave a flirty smile. "Can you tell Elgato to write more stories? We love them so much.

Rory puffed up his chest. "I'll see what I can do. Elgato is one of our most sought-after authors and doesn't send stories to any other publications."

"Are you sure?" Wes asked, wanting to keep the man talking.

Tabitha dug in her purse and retrieved her phone, then scrolled though it. "Wes did some sketches of some of Elgato's characters."

The teen girl gawked at the phone, then grabbed her boyfriend's arm. "Oh. My. God. Sappho Rueb. That's exactly how I pictured her."

Rory queued up to see the screen, and his jaw dropped as Tabitha scrolled through a few shots. Guess she was ready to throw him to the wolves but wouldn't put herself on display. He'd allow it for now.

"You did these?" The magazine editor pointed to the pictures Tabitha had taken of the sketches and then Wes. When he nodded, the man gawked.

"Have you considered selling any of these? I could get you a contract to print some of these in *Galaxia*. You're quite talented."

The teenagers hovered nearby attempting to get another peek at the pictures. "That drawing of Vared Dubrok is unbelievable. The scar on his face almost looks real. I'd definitely pay to have a print of those two sketches."

Rory handed Wes his business card. "What's your name? Are you a commercial artist?"

"Wesley Roberts. I'm in construction. I do the sketches on the side. I've been a fan of Elgato's work for a few years now and love experimenting with how I envision the work."

"This is epic," the girl said, her eyes still checking out Tabitha's phone. "You need to hook up with Elgato and do something together."

Wes surveyed the lovely redhead who was still flashing his sketching around. He'd love to hook up with her. In a completely different way than the teen girl thought.

"A collaboration with my drawings and Elgato's stories?" Wes tried for an innocent expression. "I wouldn't even know where to begin."

Rory's eyes widened as his lips split into a grin. "I have the contact information for both of you. A collaboration is an excellent suggestion. I'll have to see what I can do to make it happen."

The teenagers did little happy dances, but nothing was as beautiful as the beaming expression on Tabitha's face.

Chapter Twenty-Three

*T*abitha leaned back against the passenger head rest and closed her eyes. What she'd thought would be a day of picking out hardware for the church addition had turned into the most fun she'd had in forever. She still couldn't believe the picture she had of Wes and her with two major characters in a four-way lightsaber duel. Of course, she'd have to tuck it away so her father didn't catch a glimpse of it, but she had a feeling she'd be sneaking peeks at it for a long time.

Unless Wes wanted the picture. He'd teased about giving her storage space at his house. Was he serious? He'd paid for it after all.

Sitting up straighter, she gazed his way as he drove through traffic. "Did you want to take the picture of our lightsaber duel home with you?"

His head zipped toward her for a second, then returned to the road. "I got that for you."

"Yes, thank you so much. I don't want my father seeing it, though."

Wes patted her hand. "Keep it in the envelope and store it in your underwear drawer. He won't look in there, will he?"

"Hopefully not. If you're sure."

"I'm sure. I'm also sure I want you to get dressed up nice for dinner tonight. We're almost back at Donovan's grandparents' house."

"Dressed up? I didn't really bring anything special with me."

They pulled into the large circular driveway and stopped. Wes winked at her. "I think Maggie may have something you can borrow."

As they got out of the car, Maggie met them at the front door and let them in.

"You knew what he was planning all along, didn't you?" she accused her friend, not really upset at the unbelievable day she'd been surprised with.

Maggie tugged her up the stairs to the bedroom Tabitha had been put in, across the hall from where Wes would stay tonight.

"I brought a few dresses for you to choose from for dinner tonight. Let's take a look."

Tabitha planted her hands on her hips. "I can't believe you didn't even give me a tiny hint what he was thinking. Where are we going for dinner?"

Maggie glanced over her shoulder from where she was pulling dresses out of the closet. "I don't honestly know. He said he wanted you dressed fancy, but not ball gown fancy. Which one of these do you want?"

Tabitha perused the three dresses Maggie had grabbed from the closet. The emerald green one was a little lower cut in the cleavage than she'd ever been allowed to wear. The hem was a good few inches above her knees, as well. She'd feel downright decadent in that one.

She started to bypass that one and consider the pink sheath style, then she stopped and picked up the emerald. No one would see her.

Except Wes. He certainly wouldn't go running to her father to tattle that her dress was too short and neckline too low.

Maggie grinned and nodded. "That green dress will look stunning on you. You'll have to roll Wesley's tongue back into his mouth and his eyes back in the sockets."

"I'm not sure about that, but I'll try it on." Within minutes, Tabitha had made her decision. The dress looked stunning on her, though was still decent. In her mind if not her father's. But he wasn't here at the moment, and she really wanted Wes to be proud to be seen with her. After all he'd done for her today, it was the least she could do.

With the dress on, a pair of Maggie's spike heels borrowed, a touch of makeup, and a brush of her hair, they both headed down the stairs.

Wes and Donovan stood in the living room discussing the newest trade on some team, but Wes froze as they walked in. He looked like he'd stopped breathing.

"Are you okay?" she asked, touching his arm to get his attention. Maybe she already had it.

He thumped his fist against his chest. "Just trying to get my heart started again."

"Do you need CPR?" His pulse beat rapidly under her palm.

Donovan chuckled behind them. "A little mouth to mouth resuscitation?"

"Oh, shush, you," Maggie reprimanded her husband with a gentle pat to his arm. "Let them go have their fun, and we'll have ours while they're gone."

Tabitha whipped her head toward her friend. "Do you not want us to come back here? We can head straight to Prescott Hill."

"Of course we want you here, Tab. You're more than welcome. Go have your dinner, and don't worry about the time when you get back. I'm sure we'll see you in the morning."

"Have fun," Wes called out as he guided Tabitha out to his SUV.

Once in the car, she asked, "Where are we going?"

"I'm not sure I want to share you, looking as gorgeous as you do. I should have told you that earlier."

"I think I got the message when your jaw stuck to your chin. It's the dress. It's not my usual."

"The dress is very pretty, but it's the woman and how she's wearing it that makes it spectacular."

Heat flushed across Tabitha's face at the compliment. She hadn't heard too many in her life.

"You never said where we're going in my spectacular dress. Of course, I don't know many places in Roanoke."

"We're actually heading downriver a ways. It's about a half hour to get there. Hope that's okay."

"You gave me the perfect day, Wes. I'm not about to argue with you on anything we're doing."

"Good. What did you think of Rory Beecham? Have you ever met him before?"

Tabitha chuckled. "No, I've only dealt with him through e-mail. He knows me as T. A. Dailey. That's who the checks are made out to."

"I have a feeling you might be getting another e-mail from him soon. Perhaps requesting more stories, maybe even a collaboration with a talented new artist."

Excitement bubbled up inside. "That would be wonderful. Although do we want to go through the magazine for the graphic novel or actually put it in a print book?"

She and Wes threw around ideas for a while as they drove, regarding the book and magazine stories. When they pulled into the parking lot at a waterfront restaurant, Tabitha couldn't believe her eyes. It looked like a pirate ship.

"What in the world?"

Wes came around to open her door as she stared at the sight. "I thought you might like to be whisked away on a pirate ship for the night."

"This is incredible. How did you find this place?"

"I was doing research on what it took to be a pirate, seeing as you were so disappointed I hadn't been one in my past life. This place came up, and since it wasn't too far, I thought it might be good to take a peek."

He held out his elbow. She slipped hers through it, then they walked on what looked like the plank to get in. The inside of the restaurant did not disappoint. The lights were dim, but candles flickering on each table showed luxury tables and chairs. A stage against the back wall piqued Tabitha's curiosity.

"They have a few shows a night. Our reservation will allow us to see the first one."

At his name, the hostess led them across the room to a table near the front, then handed them some menus. Wes pulled Tabitha's chair out for her, then seated himself next to her, so they both faced the stage.

Her head was spinning at all that had happened today. This man had surprised her and then some. She still had a hard time taking it all in.

"Thank you so much, Wesley. I can't believe you did all this for me."

He shrugged. "I enjoyed it, too. The best thing about today was seeing the happiness on your face. I always want you to be happy, Tabitha."

He reached for her hand, and she allowed it, allowed his thumb to stroke her skin. The contact sent shivers up her spine, and she bit her lip to keep from showing how affected she was.

A young man appeared at the table. "I'm Patrick. I'll be your server tonight. Can I start you off with a drink?"

Tabitha wasn't a huge drinker but occasionally liked a glass of wine. "A glass of something white, please." Did that sound too ridiculous? She was hardly a wine connoisseur.

"Make that two, and we'll have the stuffed mushroom caps for an appetizer."

Patrick bobbed his head and scurried away. Tabitha peered at Wesley. "How did you know I love stuffed mushrooms?"

"You always get them whenever someone makes them at the potluck. I've seen the way you look longingly at people's plates if they run out before you get there. I hope it wasn't too presumptuous of me to order them. We can order something else."

"No, that's perfect."

She reviewed the menu for her main meal. It had a good variety of cuisine, and she couldn't decide what she wanted. Too many dishes made her mouth water. Should she get a tried and true or something she'd never allowed herself? After all the new activities today, the choice seemed obvious.

When their appetizer arrived, she ordered braised short ribs with Parmesan mashed potatoes and grilled vegetables. Wesley got a ribeye steak, baked potato, and vegetables.

He scooped a mushroom onto a small plate for each of them and handed one to her. The stuffing was heavenly, and she couldn't stop herself from groaning out loud. Wes laughed but agreed once he'd taken a bite of his.

"Oh, hey, I forgot to tell you," she said. "Remember the Handlers, that family I was telling you about that lost their house?"

Wes only paused in his chewing for a second to nod.

"Apparently, some good Samaritan bought the foreclosure and is renting it back to them for a small monthly fee."

"That's great, isn't it?" He tipped his head.

"It's wonderful. They have no idea who it is, though. They found out through a lawyer who offered to have them move back in. They've also been given the option to buy back the house when they save up enough money."

"It's too bad they have to go through all this to begin with."

"I agree. That horrible bank manager should be strung up with what he did to that poor family. Now, they've got a second chance due to a guardian angel out there. I wish I knew who it was."

"Why? Do you need a guardian angel?"

Her face heated. "I know my situation isn't anywhere as bad as the Handler's, but I'd love a little guidance in finding a good job, one that allows me time to write, and an apartment."

"You're determined to live in the city, huh?"

"I am. Mostly to be away from my father. I'd have plenty of time, since I'm hardly a party girl every night. I just need a good job."

Wes tipped his chin at the female pirates currently crossing the stage. "You could always get a job here as a pirate wench."

Chapter Twenty-Four

Tabitha pushed her way into Kayla's apartment and placed a pizza box on the kitchen table. In seconds, she had two slices of extra cheese slapped on a plate and was hightailing it to the balcony. The view of the river was astounding and always calmed her.

Kayla, Maggie, and Aubrey joined her moments later, their own pizza and drinks in hand.

"Does Miss Tabitha Dailey have any news to report from her two days away with the shaggy-haired boy?" Aubrey pushed her overlarge sunglasses to the top of her head. "There were too many people around at the potluck to get the juicy details."

Tabitha glared at her friend. "Maggie was with us. She could have provided you with details."

"Oh, no no." Maggie waved her hand in the air, her pizza almost flying off the plate. "Donovan and I were only with Miss Dailey and the shaggy-haired boy for lunch on Friday. We saw them again for a short time Saturday morning before we split up to go our separate ways."

Kayla peered over her glass of sweet tea. "Which way would that have been, Miss Dailey?"

Tabitha knew she'd have to spill the beans about the weekend but had to at least play hard to get first. She munched on her pizza, took a few sips of her drink, then sighed.

"Wesley and I bought hardware for the church addition at some stores in Roanoke."

All three friends glared. Tabitha laughed.

"After we had lunch with the lovely Mr. and Mrs. Sinclair, we took a stroll down the street to the Berglund Center, where there so happened to be a science fiction convention, though I believe Mrs. Magnolia Sinclair was aware of this event."

Maggie snarfed her pizza and averted her eyes. Kayla and Aubrey hid grins. Had they known Wes was bringing her there, too? If so, they'd kept it well hidden.

"How was the convention? Who did you see? I heard that sexy Aquaman was going to be there."

"He was. Wes and I got a picture of us having a lightsaber fight with him and another actor." Aubrey wasn't into any of the *star* shows and movies, so mentioning names wouldn't mean anything to her.

Her friend's eyes popped open, and her mouth turned down. "Maybe I need to start watching this science fiction stuff."

"Did you have fun?" Kayla asked.

Tabitha sagged back in her chair and closed her eyes for a moment, remembering how terrific it had been. "I can't even describe how much. We saw several panels with the cast of a few different shows. We got the picture taken and then autographed later. But one of the best things that happened was when we were walking around the auditorium where all the vendors were. *Galaxia* magazine was there."

Tabitha filled them in on meeting her editor, the teens who were fanning all over Tempus Elgato, and the discussion regarding Wesley's sketches and a possible collaboration.

"Wait, did you tell them you're Tempus Elgato?" Aubrey sat up and squinted at her.

"No, I didn't want to do it there. Too awkward, and I had no proof. They might have thought I was lying. However, I got an e-mail this week from Rory, the editor, and he wants to set up a video call to discuss some future plans."

"Ooh, sounds promising," Maggie squealed, shimmying in her seat. "Are you going to do a collaboration with Wes?"

"I told you we've already started work on a graphic novel with sketches he's done. I may mention that when I get a chance to talk to this guy."

Aubrey leaned back and crossed her arms. "So maybe Wes isn't such a bad guy after all."

Definitely not a bad guy. "I never said he was. Just not for me."

Kayla frowned. "Still? Even with all you two have in common? What about his geek side?"

"His geek side is unbelievable and totally cool, but I still want out of this town. This weekend only showed me how much more there is than this little suburb."

Aubrey held her hands to her ears. "Stop talking about leaving us. I won't let you."

Tabitha reached out and squeezed her friend's arm. "I'll always be around if you need me, sweetie." Aubrey's home life hadn't been the best, and guilt burned through her when Aubrey slid her glasses down and leaned back on her chair.

"Come on, Tab," Maggie said, "You don't like him even a tiny bit? I find that hard to believe. I saw you with him this weekend."

"Fine. I like him. A lot. Maybe more than a lot. I confess that working on this collaboration with him may have eased the doldrums of my life, though hasn't made my job any more exciting."

"How's Mrs. Chavez working out?" Kayla brought out the pizza box and passed it around. Aubrey took two more pieces and chowed them down. Seemed the more Aubrey ate, the thinner she got.

"That woman is a godsend. She's taken on pretty much everything in the office. I've even set up a smaller desk in the back of my office, and I'm using that while she's at my desk doing all my work."

Maggie licked sauce off her fingers. "Then, what are you doing while you're there?"

"She thinks I'm typing up Dad's backlog of sermons that he's got handwritten from years ago. He's been thinking of putting them together in a book to publish. Naturally, it's fine for him to publish something, but not me."

Aubrey crooked her head. "You said she *thinks* you're typing the sermons. What are you actually doing? Your graphic novel with Wes?"

Tabitha shook her head. "Most of the text for that is in at least rough draft form. He needs to catch up with his sketches before we do any revisions. I've started weaving all my magazine stories together into a novel. Wes loves the idea and encouraged me to do it."

"He's been super supportive, hasn't he?" Kayla said. "You haven't wanted to move to anything more than friends?"

Did she? Kind of, yet she'd been balking at his advances for so long she wasn't sure how to let him know maybe he should try again.

"It may have crossed my mind a time or two. Especially when we're sitting so close, working on the collaboration or discussing something. He smells so good."

Aubrey straightened up and lifted her sunglasses. "Miss Dailey is sniffing the shaggy-haired boy now? Is that appropriate?"

Tabitha laughed. She loved her friends and how outrageous they could be.

Maggie narrowed her eyes. "Have you kissed yet? Any shenanigans? We didn't hear anything while at Donovan's grandparents' house."

"That's because he hasn't done more than kiss my cheek or my forehead. He's been a perfect gentleman."

Kayla's lips twisted into a grimace. "That's too bad."

Wesley heard a car pull up his drive and ran to the front door. He really needed to get his driveway graded so Tabitha wasn't rattling around when she stopped by. Which she'd done often lately. In the past two weeks, since he'd surprised her with the trip to the science fiction convention, she'd visited every few days to work on their collaboration. What she was telling her father, he had no idea.

"Hey there, pretty lady. I was about to put steaks on the grill. Hungry?"

"You spoil me. I won't be able to go back to rice and beans again."

He guided her into the house, admiring the cut off jean shorts and tank top. Obviously, she'd peeled off a layer since leaving home.

Once inside, a scuffling noise caught her attention. Wes couldn't wait to see her face at his newest surprise.

"What is that noise? It almost sounds like a—"

The tiny yip from the box in the sunken living room was unmistakable. Her eyes rounded on him, and her mouth fell open. "Did you get a dog?"

He shrugged and trotted over to the box, then pulled out the collie stumbling around inside. When he held it up, tears filled her eyes.

"It's Lassie. You got a Lassie dog." Suddenly, her face tightened, and she frowned.

"I thought that was the kind of dog you liked." Had he misunderstood her?

"It is. But it's your dog, not mine."

Holding the puppy closer to Tabitha's face, he said, "You can visit him any time you like. Mi puppy es su puppy."

"Can I hold him?" She bit her lip as the little guy squirmed in Wesley's arms.

"Sit on the floor, and he'll crawl in your lap. He's got an abundance of energy."

Tabitha lowered herself to the floor near the crate, and Wes deposited the dog next to her. Immediately, he scampered around the room, then loped back toward the beautiful redhead. As the animal jumped and licked at her face, Tabitha threw her head back and let out a belly laugh. The joy in her expression was a sight to see. One he wanted to see forever.

Was he seriously thinking of marriage with her? They hadn't even officially dated. Didn't matter. He'd been in love with this woman since shortly after he'd met her. During the last two years, and the past five months working on the addition, his love had grown deeper than ever. All he had to do was make sure she loved him, too.

"When did you decide to get a dog?" Tabitha scratched the puppy behind his ears, and the little guy's tail thumped a rapid beat.

"I'd been thinking about one for a while. Since moving in here, anyway. Obviously, I couldn't really get one while living in Maggie's bunkhouse. I've got a great yard here, and I'm all by myself. He'll be good company when I don't have visitors." He'd been hoping Tabitha would want to visit him constantly.

"What'll you do with him when you're working?" Her eyes grew concerned.

"I bought a small playpen and figured he can play inside that under the shade of that big live oak tree for now. Do you think your father will have a problem with that? I suppose I could get a babysitter for him. Maybe the person who watches Big Mama Prescott's darling."

They both laughed, and Tabitha scooped the dog into her lap for more scratches.

"He's still so small; he'll probably be fine. By the time he's bigger, you'll most likely have the addition finished."

"True. And once I become a famous science fiction artist making boatloads of money, I can stay home."

Her head tipped to the side as she grinned. "If you're making boatloads of money on your art, then I want to make boatloads of money on my books."

Wes stuck his hand out. "Deal. We both make boatloads of money." When would be the best time to tell her he already had boatloads of money? Even though he knew she wasn't any kind of gold digger, he wanted to make sure she felt the same about him as he did about her.

Her sigh drifted across the room. "If only it were that easy. Though I did get an e-mail from Rory yesterday, asking if we could do a video call. Hopefully, you put a bug in his ear about our collaboration."

"I didn't put a bug in his ear. You showed him my drawings, then those teenagers jumped in with enthusiasm for the project. Right place, right time."

She shrugged. "It may not be anything big. He might just want more short stories from Tempus. I'm not getting my hopes up until I talk to him."

The dog jumped up and down, then snuggled into Tabitha's chest. Lucky dog.

"You know, if you bring him to the church, I can probably take him for a few walks if he needs it. Especially now that Mrs. Chavez is taking everything over. I really need to do something super special for Aubrey for suggesting that."

Wes got on the floor next to Tabitha and ran his hand over the puppy's back. She was so close and smelled so good. Her face glowed as she watched the animal in her lap.

He sighed and she peeked at him, her lips twisted in a smile. "So lovely."

Her gaze stayed on his as he eased in closer, her lips only a whisper away from his. He wanted to kiss her so badly it was almost as if he could taste it. Closer. Closer.

Woof! The puppy scampered on her lap and jumped up between them, licking both their faces. Wes pulled back and frowned, though not for long. The adorable dog was too cute, and Tabitha's excitement at holding him couldn't be erased.

"This little guy needs a name. What do you think we should call him?"

Tabitha tilted her head. "We? It's your dog. Why would I choose a name?"

"I expect you to help me with him whenever you're around. Any suggestions?"

"What if I choose something horrible? Can you trust me with that kind of decision?"

Wes picked up the pup and held it near her face. "You wouldn't do that to an adorable puppy like this, would you?"

"No, but I might pick something fussy and ridiculous."

Wes shook his head. "You aren't the fussy and ridiculous type, Tabitha. It's one of the things I really like about you." He wanted to name off all the other things he liked about her, but that would have to wait for another time.

"How about Buttercup?" she said with a gleam in her eye. "To go with the farm boy."

He pursed his lips, though he could tell she was kidding. "He might have a problem with Buttercup. Something a little more masculine perhaps."

Tabitha stroked the dog's fur and ran her finger over the dark spot around his eye. "Hmm. Looks a little like an eye patch. I think we should name him Pirate."

Wes let out a loud chuckle. "I love it. Pirate it is."

Chapter Twenty-Five

*T*abitha tapped her foot and waited for the video call from Rory Beecham to connect. Fortunately, it was her father's night to lead Bible study. Mrs. Chavez had offered to help him run it and that had seemed to distract him enough that he hadn't asked what her plans were.

Her laptop hummed, and finally the screen showed the man's face. A very perplexed face.

"T.A. Dailey?"

"Yes, I'm Tabitha Dailey or Tempus Elgato in the writing world."

"It's nice to finally meet you, though I'm a little surprised. Why didn't you introduce yourself a few weeks ago at the science fiction convention?"

Tabitha lifted a shoulder. "There were lots of people around. I'd like to keep my identity a secret for now, if you don't mind."

The man nodded, his lips pulled together. "Of course. You aren't the first person to use a pen name. I'm curious about your friend who does the sketches. He's extremely talented."

"He is. We've actually started working on a collaboration."

"Because of the conversation at the convention?"

Tabitha shook her head. "No, we began a few months ago. We can talk about that later if you want. What was the reason you wanted to have a face-to-face chat today?"

Rory grinned. "Your stories have done well in the magazine. Issues with them always sell out quickly. I was hoping to talk you into providing us with more, as you only have two left for publication."

"I'm always interested in getting more of my stories out there. But I have to tell you that all of these have a connection, if you hadn't figured it out. I'm in the process of piecing them together into a novel. I'm not sure exactly what I'm going to do with it, but hopefully get it published somewhere."

"Well, Miss Dailey, I've got connections at one of the publishing houses that specializes in science fiction and fantasy. I've helped more than a few authors who started in *Galaxia* to branch out into novels. I'd be happy to introduce you to the editor-in-chief there."

"Seriously?" Tabitha almost squealed with excitement but managed to hold it together long enough to get coherent words out. "That would be most welcome, Mr. Beecham."

"Rory was fine the other day. It's fine now. I want to talk to you about providing more content for *Galaxia*. Do you have any works that aren't related to the novel you're putting together?"

"Wesley Roberts and I have started work on a graphic novel together. That's new content, but it's an entire continuous story. It's not split into standalone pieces like I've been giving you before. I can probably write something else if that's what you're looking for. I don't know when I'll have it, since I don't want to let Wesley down, not to mention I have a real-world job as well."

"I'd be very interested in seeing the graphic novel and incorporating it into the magazine. With your name, it will pull readers in."

"But we want to make it a book." Were they hoping for too much with their project?

"You still can. What I suggest is to start the graphic novel in the magazine. We do a few-page spread every other issue. We get readers hooked, then they'll want to buy the book to continue the story."

Her head spun. "You'd be willing to do that?"

Rory grinned. "Are you kidding me? It's a great way to get people buying the magazine, and it's free advertising for you."

"I see that."

"You're very talented, and Tempus Elgato has made a name for himself. Uh, herself. Themself. I have a feeling you'll be going places with this pen name and your writing. With a little help. The issues that have your stories are always our highest selling ones. I'm happy to start a series in the magazine and provide that free promotion."

"Won't people get mad if they start a series in the magazine and can't get the whole story there?"

"Right now, all your stories are written as standalones, so there're no cliffhangers and everyone is satisfied with the end. Even if we start a series where each episode is continued in the next issue, it'll be less expensive for someone to buy the entire book than to keep paying for every issue of the magazine."

"I know, but what's in it for the magazine? Why would you do this for us?"

"Because you're going to keep providing us with fresh content. I'd like to draw up a contract for both you and Mr. Roberts. I'd love to put some of his sketches in with your stories. I can guarantee those issues will sell like hotcakes. Then, I want to work out a schedule for the graphic novel and how many episodes we'll print before the book comes out."

This was all moving way too fast for Tabitha. "But we don't have a contract for the graphic novel yet."

"How far along are you in the development phase?"

"The storyline is fleshed out with a rough draft of the text. We know what each of the illustrations will be, but Wes only has about half of them outlined."

"I'm going to give you the name of someone, and I want you to send him a synopsis of the novel and the illustrations for the first chapter. They can be rough draft. He just needs to see the skill level of the artist. Can you do that?"

"I can. It may take about a week to get it all together, though. Will that be too late?"

Rory laughed. "He doesn't even know you're sending them yet. I'll give him a buzz tomorrow and tell him what's coming his way. I'll also let him know that we'll be introducing the novel in *Galaxia,* and he and I can work out details on scheduling."

"That's if he wants to publish the graphic novel, right?"

"True. I can't speak for him, but we've done this kind of thing before, and he usually trusts my judgment. At the very least, I can guarantee a contract for the graphic novel in *Galaxia.* How it goes from there to finished print product can be discussed later. If that sounds workable, I'll have my assistant draw up another contract and send it to you."

"Yes, thank you so much."

"Thank you, Tabitha. I have a feeling we'll be doing a lot more work together very soon."

As the video shut down, Tabitha let out a long squeal, thankful her father wasn't in the house. She had to tell Wes right away. What did this mean for her getaway plans? She still had money saved up to move to the city, but would she and Wes be able to work together if she lived in Roanoke and he lived here?

It was too much to think about. She'd pushed Wesley away for so long, even when she'd wanted to hold him close. Could she start rethinking her goals?

Ideas formed in her mind as she jumped in the car and drove out to the log cabin.

Pirate yapped away as a car rolled up to Wesley's house. He wasn't expecting anyone. Tabitha had given a wave as she'd hurried from the church office to her house but hadn't stopped to chat, so he'd gathered up his tools and the puppy once his work was done and gone home.

However, that was Tabitha's car stopping in front of his house. After putting a yipping Pirate into his crate, Wes hustled out to the porch and down the steps. He'd barely reached the yard when she barreled toward him and flung herself in his arms. All right then.

"I have such great news," she gushed and eased back from his shoulder. Her beaming face was so gorgeous, her lips turned up in a huge smile.

Those lips were too much for him to have any kind of control. Stroking one side of her face, he lowered his mouth to hers. The touch of her lips to his created a whirlwind inside him. He pressed them together again and again, sweetly and gently, though he wanted to plunder. But he wouldn't with Tabitha, no matter how much she'd joked about being swept away by a pirate.

After kissing her for several perfect moments, far less time than he wanted, he lifted his eyes, his forehead still glued to hers.

A soft sigh floated from her mouth. "Lust."

"What?"

Her dreamy eyes fluttered open, and blush colored her cheeks. "Oh, I'm sorry. Just those Seven Deadly Sins again. I've been working my way through them for a while now. Hadn't gotten to lust yet."

"Until now?"

She bit her lip. "Until now. I've only got a couple left."

Her hair under his fingers felt like silk. "Since you've already committed the sin, can we engage a bit more?"

A sly smile crossed her face. The tongue that ran across her bottom lip told him to continue. So he did.

Every feeling he'd ever had regarding Tabitha grew to enormous proportions as he touched his mouth to hers. He stroked his hand down her hair, then cupped her cheek. Her shy response was telling, and he wondered what was wrong with the guys in her life that no one had ever appreciated her enough to ask her out. He certainly wouldn't make that mistake.

"Maybe I've never said it, but I care about you, Tabitha. A lot. I haven't even thought of another woman since I met you. I want to make sure you know how I feel."

She glanced at the ground, then peered up at him. "I'm getting kind of used to you, too."

"Does that mean you'll go out on a date with me?" Strike while the iron was hot. And man, that kiss, even as sweet as it was, was hot.

Tabitha laughed, and he wasn't sure if he should be relieved or insulted.

"What was all that stuff we did a few weeks ago? The convention? Dinner? Holding hands while we took a walk?"

"I hoped, but I didn't want to presume. A few times we've done stuff, and you were very clear—they weren't dates."

Her gaze roamed past him, then back again. "I didn't say the Roanoke day events weren't dates."

"You didn't say they were." He caressed her cheek with his thumb, and she shivered. A good shiver, hopefully. "Can I take you out around here, in Prescott Hill? With all the locals seeing us together?"

"Be seen with you in public?" There was a twinkle in her eyes. He loved this mischievous side to her. "I could allow it."

"And I'd tell your father I'm taking you out."

"My father? You're sure you want to deal with him?"

"I do. Will I have to fill out a questionnaire? Give a blood sample and fingerprints?" He'd do that for her.

"I honestly don't know. Aside from a few guys in college, I've never dated much. Never boys from town."

Heat flashed across his face. "Are all the men in town idiots?"

She smirked. "Either idiots or cowards. They don't want to deal with my father."

He'd deal with anyone he had to, if it meant he had Tabitha's arms around him. Like they still were now. She hadn't let go, and he didn't want her to.

"I'm happy to talk to him if you want me to."

A silly grin made her appear younger. "I suppose he can hardly run you out of town. He wants his addition finished."

"That's good to know. Seriously, though, I want to continue seeing you. Not just to collaborate on the graphic novel. Maybe do more of this."

He kissed her again, and when her arms tightened around his neck, he gave a silent cheer. Thank God for whatever had brought her running over here in such a mood. They'd never gotten around to discussing it.

One more kiss, and he loosened his grip. "What were you so excited about when you got here?"

Her mouth formed a perfect bow. "Oh, how did I forget?"

"Maybe this." He kissed her again.

"Definitely that. I wanted to tell you I had that video call with Rory Beecham. He's very interested in your drawings."

"My drawings? Why did he call you, then?"

"He didn't originally call about your artwork, but when he saw who I was, that topic came up. He wants more content from Tempus Elgato."

"Beyond the two stories they already have?"

"Yes. I mentioned the collaboration you and I are doing on a graphic novel, and he wants to put those in the magazine, too."

"I thought we planned to do a print book."

"We do. He had a suggestion." Tabitha detailed what Beecham had suggested and mentioned the publisher friend who could potentially help them get the book in print.

"So, what does he get from this deal? Sounds too good to be true."

She bit her bottom lip and nodded. "That's what I thought, too. He said he gets more content for the magazine. Apparently, Tempus is a fan favorite."

"I already told you she's my favorite. In many ways."

He cupped her face and pressed his lips to her again. The sigh she exhaled gave him so much hope.

Chapter Twenty-Six

*T*abitha patted the documents on the seat next to her as she maneuvered toward Wesley's. The contract for her new Tempus Elgato stories. There had been a note from Rory, stating he'd sent a contract to Wesley, as well, for some of the illustrations that went with her world.

The excitement she felt was almost too much, and she wondered if her bubble would pop soon. Something would happen so her stories didn't go any further, and she was stuck in her secretary world forever.

As she pulled up the driveway, her heart almost stopped. Smoke poured from the back of the house. It was far too much to be his grill, unless he'd doused it with gasoline. She slammed on the brakes, put it in park, and hotfooted it into the house. Thankfully, the front door was unlocked.

Smoke filled the hallway and seemed to come from the kitchen.

"Wesley? Where are you?" Her voice sounded strange even to her ears. Where was he? Injured? Worse? No, he couldn't be.

"Tabitha, take him and try and calm him down." Wes shoved Pirate into her hands, then disappeared into the smoke again. Something clanged, then the sound of a fire extinguisher echoed through the room.

The puppy's heart was beating frantically, almost as fast as hers. "It's okay, Pirate. You're okay." She backed away and opened the front door to vent the smoke but didn't go much farther. She wanted to make sure Wes was all right.

"Do you need help?" Her hand stroked the dog's head and ears, attempting to calm the poor little guy. What in the world had happened?

Inspecting the animal, she ascertained he hadn't been burned. He was merely scared. She couldn't blame him. She was terrified.

Wes appeared, waving a small dishtowel at the smoke that remained. He'd opened the slider to the back deck and turned on the exhaust fan on the stove.

"Is he okay? I couldn't see enough with the flames and smoke to check."

She rubbed the adorable pup. "He seems okay, just frightened. What in the world happened?"

Wes led her to the front porch and nodded at the swing. He dropped next to her and sighed.

"I wasn't paying close enough attention to Pirate, and he jumped up when I was pouring some olive oil into a pan. It splashed onto the flames. Consequences of a gas stove, I guess. I was more worried about the dog than the fire, and a few dish towels caught on fire, as well. That's when you showed up, thankfully."

Moving the dog to one arm, she reached for his hands. "Did you get burned at all?"

He winced when she touched a red spot on the side of his fingers. "A bit. It's not too bad."

"Hold him." She placed Pirate in his lap and trotted into the kitchen. Oh, no. The fire had caused damage to some of the wall board and part of a cabinet. Quickly, she found another towel, wet it with cold water, and grabbed some ice cubes, folding them inside to keep the towel cool.

Outside again, she wrapped the towel around his fingers and took the dog back. "Keep that wet. They don't look too awful, but I'm hardly a doctor. If they're still bad in a little while, we should get you to the hospital."

"They're fine, Tabitha. It's only a few tiny spots. The cold water already seems to be helping."

"We'll need to keep cold water on them for a while. Once the ice cubes inside the towel have all melted, I'll soak that again and add a few more."

"You'd be a great little nurse. Ever thought about going back to school?"

"I have a degree. Two, actually. In theology and literature. I've never been one for math and science, so nursing was always out."

"I'm sure your literature degree helped when you started writing."

She laughed. "It didn't get me involved in writing science fiction, but it helped me know grammar and punctuation and how to plot a story."

"All good things. How's the little pup doing?"

Pirate had snuggled in her lap and seemed to be asleep. "Better now. Poor thing must have been scared."

Wes grimaced. "I should have been watching him better. Or put him in his crate while I cooked. I'll have to do that until I can train him not to jump up on people. Hopefully, the kitchen isn't in too bad a shape."

Tabitha pictured what she'd seen when she got the towels. There was extensive damage to some of the areas. "Listen, I've got money saved. I was planning to use it to move to Roanoke, but things have changed recently. I want you to have it. Use it to fix up the kitchen."

Wes narrowed his eyes. "You want to give me all your savings? You don't need to do that."

"I want to. I know you lowballed the church addition bid. I'm not sure why, but it got you the contract. You can't be making much profit once you purchase all the materials. I won't even mention how much you pay Maggie's kids when they help you."

"You did just mention that I pay them." His lips quirked to the side.

"I didn't say how much. Regardless, I know you aren't getting a huge profit from this contract. Your kitchen is going to need some work. I want to help pay for it."

Wes took a deep breath and held it. Slowly, he released it and stared at her. "Tabitha, you are so sweet and generous, but I don't need your money. I have plenty."

"I know. You said you saved some from your previous job, but there can't be that much left after building this house."

"I have a trust fund. My grandmother left me plenty after she passed away. It's what I've been using to pay for the house. It's one of the reasons I bid so low on the church addition. I enjoy the work. I don't really need it."

Tabitha stilled on the seat. "You don't have to work? You have enough money in this trust fund to live on for a while?" How did she feel about this? How had she not known this? Did anyone in town know?

"I do. As long as I don't go crazy and buy multi-million-dollar houses and jets, I could live comfortably on it for the rest of my life."

She peered closer at him. "The rest of your life? That's quite a bit of money. What did your grandmother do to get this fortune?"

"A good deal of it was family money, but my grandfather still has his hand in the business world and makes sure my trust fund makes good interest."

"I thought your grandfather was a carpenter who taught you how to build."

"That was my dad's father. My mother came from money. My grandmother, Viveca Lipton, was wealthy in her own right even before she married my grandfather."

"Lipton? Wait. Arthur Lipton? He's that horrible banker from Roanoke who stole the Handler's house from them. Is he any relation?" Hopefully not.

Wes paled, his fingers clenching in Pirate's fur. "He's my grandfather."

Scooting the pup all the way into Wesley's lap, Tabitha jumped to her feet. "You're related to that money-grubbing banker who thinks it's fun to rip people's houses out from under them when something tiny comes along to derail them."

"Unfortunately. I don't really talk to him much."

"Just when you have to get money for your house. Here I thought you were some struggling carpenter, just an average Joe. But you're up there in the same category as the Prescotts and the Sinclairs, right?"

"I guess."

"You never thought it prudent to let me in on this little fact? You allowed me to feel bad for you because you weren't making a good paycheck from the church addition."

Wes got to his feet, Pirate still clutched in his arms. "I never said anything about not making enough money from the addition. That was all in your head."

"It's all in my head. How many women have heard that before?"

"Tabitha, look, I never mentioned the trust fund because too many people only want to be friends when you have money."

"You thought I'd be one of them?" What had she ever done to make him think that? Okay, her comments about living in the city might have been a tiny indication, but she'd never be friends with someone simply because of wealth. The implication wounded her.

"No, I never said that."

"You didn't say a lot of things, Wesley."

"Would it have changed things if you knew how much money I had?" His expression was one of hurt.

"I don't care about the money. I do care that you basically lied to me. When I mentioned the Handler's house, that would have been the perfect time to let me know Lipton was your grandfather."

"Oh, sure. You talk about this man who you loathe and what a horrible person he is, then I jump in with being spawned from him. Can't imagine that would have kept the river floating stress free and relaxing."

"I've worried about you and how you could afford this house for a long time. If I had known you had a trust fund, maybe I wouldn't have been so anxious. I don't know, Wes. Perhaps I've been hanging out at church too long because the truth is extremely important to me. I've got to go."

"Wait. When will I see you again?"

The thought he'd kept information of this magnitude from her after how close they'd gotten lately heated her blood. "I don't know if you will."

As she stormed off to her car, she knew she'd just committed the last of the Seven Deadly Sins. Wrath.

Chapter Twenty-Seven

*A*fter parking in town, Wes trotted on the sidewalk until he reached the building Donovan Sinclair rented for his business. He didn't have an appointment, and the sign said they were closing in twenty minutes. Hopefully, his friend would have time for him.

Donovan sat at a desk, gazing at his computer screen, then glanced up when Wes tapped on the door. His friend waved him in and stood to shake hands.

"Wes, nice surprise. What are you doing in town? You done for the day at the church?"

"Done, yeah. Do you mind if I sit? Are you on your way out?"

Donovan glanced at his watch and indicated the chair across from him, then sat back down. "I was just doing some research for a new client. Maggie's got her ladies' night at Kayla's place. They do pizza and gab for a few hours. I assume you know the drill since Tabitha always attends, too."

Wes inhaled deeply and released it quickly. "I don't even want to know what they're gabbing about tonight. I have a feeling it'll be me. And not in a good way."

Donovan raised one eyebrow. "What did you do?"

"I didn't do anything. It's more something I didn't tell Tabitha. We had a fight yesterday, and she stormed out. She avoided me the entire day today at the church and made up all sorts of errands that needed to be run so she could be out of the office."

"I've got a good set of ears if you want to get it off your chest."

Donovan was a good friend. Wes wasn't one to go around sharing his woes, but he could use some advice from another guy who'd needed to do some groveling at one point. Donovan had groveled with the best of them to win Maggie's heart.

"You know I've had a thing for Tabitha since I moved into town a few years ago."

"So Maggie tells me."

"There's just something about her that sends my heart racing. She ticks off every box I've ever had regarding women, and we connect on a level I'd never experienced before. Especially in the last five months. She wanted nothing to do with me for so long, but finally she agreed to start dating."

"Start dating? You hadn't been dating? What about the trip to Roanoke?"

Wes threaded his fingers through his hair. "I wanted that to be a date, and I guess Tabitha kind of considered them dates, too. But a few weeks ago, we talked, and she agreed to actually let people know we were together."

"Then, this thing you forgot to tell her came up and bit you in the behind."

"Yeah. See, she's had this image of me as a down-on-your-luck guy who barely gets by. She knows what my bid was for the church addition, and she's smart enough to realize I wouldn't make much of a profit once I purchased the materials and paid Maggie's kids for some of the labor. I let her know I had some money saved from a previous job, but she still worried because she's beautiful like that."

"So you either have less money than you hinted at or more."

Wes sighed. "More. A lot more."

Donovan tipped his head. "She has a problem with you having money? Strange, but not a bad thing. I've had plenty of women want to date me simply because of my family's wealth."

"Yeah, I've been there, too. It doesn't feel good."

"I assume your money is family money, then."

"Yeah, and that's kind of where the problem arises. Do you know the Handlers in town?"

Donovan squinted. "Handlers. Sounds familiar. Wait. The family who lost their house recently. Maggie mentioned something about wanting to help them. Are you related to them?"

"No. I bought the mortgage from the bank and am renting it back to them for less than they were paying before. I'm putting the money they pay me into an account and will use it toward the price of the house when I sell it back to them. They don't know about that yet."

"Wow, that's quite generous of you. How does this have anything to do with why Tabitha is upset with you?"

"Because the banker who called in the loan prematurely, without giving the Handlers the chance to pay up the back amount owed, is Arthur Lipton. My grandfather."

Easing back in his chair, Donovan steepled his hands. "Ah, Lipton. I've heard of him. Not many good things, though I suppose some would say he's a shrewd businessman."

"A real cold fish who doesn't care about anything except money. I don't have a whole lot to do with him. I considered pleading the Handler's case with him, but I knew I'd end up owing him something I wasn't willing to give. It was far less expensive to buy the mortgage through an agent and allow them to continue living there."

"Your grandfather doesn't know you bought it?"

"Nope. I don't plan to ever tell him either."

"I can't imagine Tabitha was upset because you bought the Handler's house. That doesn't make sense."

"I haven't told her about that. Maybe I should and she'll forgive me my other transgression, which was not telling her who my grandfather was. She mentioned him a few times when the Handlers first got foreclosed on. The way she spoke about him didn't give me confidence that telling her would be a good thing. Not at the time."

Tipping his chin up, Donovan pointed to Wes. "What did you need from me?"

"Advice on how to win her back. I heard enough about your background with Magnolia to know there was some groveling involved. I wanted to know if you had any suggestions."

His friend laughed. "My situation was a little different. My transgression was years ago. Once I was able to get close enough to Maggie, I apologized."

"That's all it took?"

"That and a month of mucking out stalls and feeding the chickens. When she realized I'd do anything for her, including moving back to Prescott Hill, she finally admitted she had feelings, too. What is something Tabitha wants?"

"She wants adventure and to get away from this small town. I'd be happy to take her anywhere she wants to go, but she's far too practical to allow that. She's not a gold digger. I never said anything about my trust fund because I didn't want people to like me for my money."

Donovan nodded, frowning. "I completely understand that. And you're right, Tabitha's not like that. It's why she and Maggie are such good friends. There must be something you can offer her, once you apologize for keeping the grandfather thing from her."

"I tried to apologize, but she kept avoiding me today. It's like I went back in time to before I started the addition." Wesley ran his hands over his face, thinking of the things he'd done to try and win her over. "She's always loved science fiction, so I brought her to that convention."

"I think she enjoyed that. She raved to Maggie about how much fun it was."

Wes dipped his chin. "I also bought a puppy. She's never had a dog and wished she could have gotten one."

"Did you get the puppy for her or for you?"

Wes glanced at the ceiling. "Well, I like the little guy, but I admit my motives were hardly pure of heart. I wanted to get her something she'd always dreamed of and her father wouldn't let her have. I thought it might make me look better in her eyes, and she'd be willing to give me a chance. Let's face it, she's been avoiding me for almost two years."

"Not lately," Donovan pointed out.

"No, because I've been working at the church every day, and then we found we had this science fiction fantasy connection."

"Maggie mentioned you've been working on a story together. I know I'm not supposed to know about Tabitha's alter ego, but I swore to Maggie I'd keep it to myself. I'm assuming you know if you're collaborating with her. It sounds like you have a connection to her with this graphic novel you're both working on."

"True, but I want to connect with her on every level, not just the science fiction one."

Donovan shrugged. "If Tabitha is serious about her writing, and Maggie says she is, then she'd be foolish to give it all up just because she's upset with you. Give her a few days to really think about what you did and why you did it. She's an intelligent woman, Wes. I think you'll find she'll come to the conclusion that you didn't set out to hurt her all on her own. Throwing in an apology and some flowers or candy won't hurt either."

"Or I could get Mrs. Mancini to make one of her rhubarb pies and give it to her. She never gets to the buffet table at the potluck early enough to get any."

"They say the way to a man's heart is through his stomach. Maybe it's the same for women. Especially if it involves Mrs. Mancini's rhubarb pie."

Wesley hoped it was true. He had to convince Mrs. Mancini to make him a pie. He had a feeling if he confessed it was for true love, she'd be happy to do it.

Chapter Twenty-Eight

*K*ayla plopped a slice of pepperoni pizza onto a paper plate and gave Tabitha a searching look. "What got in your bonnet this time, Miss Dailey?"

Aubrey pursed her mulberry stained lips. "Yeah, you've been so happy lately. What happened to put a damper on that?"

"Wesley." She couldn't say more right now, so she shoved her slice of pizza in her mouth and chewed vigorously.

"Oh, dear," Kayla groaned. "What did he do? Do we need to hurt him? I won't break a nail, but my brothers would do some damage if I asked."

Tabitha thought of the burns on Wesley's hands and felt bad she hadn't asked if they were still hurting today at work. She'd hardly even been there. With Mrs. Chavez in the office, she'd been freed up to run all sorts of errands she ordinarily had to wait to do until after work or weekends. Her father hadn't even said anything about her being absent most of the day.

Tabitha filled them in on the conversation she'd had with Wesley and who his grandfather was.

"So what?" Maggie said. "His grandfather is a nasty person. So is my mother-in-law. You can't choose your relatives."

"It's not because of who his grandfather is. He lied to me. Never told me who he was and that I didn't need to worry about him having enough money to pay his bills."

Aubrey pushed her sunglasses to the edge of her nose. "Can you really call it lying? He didn't give up the information, but it's not like you asked him who his grandfather was and he told you something that wasn't true."

"Would you want to fess up to being related to someone as awful as Arthur Lipton after what you've heard about the man?" Kayla asked.

Tabitha could hardly argue with her friends. She'd been judged for years because she was the preacher's daughter. So many people had preconceived notions of who she was based on her father and his position in the church.

"Probably not. I may have jumped the gun a little, but it hurt that he didn't trust me enough to tell me. Or worse, he thought I'd only want him if he had money."

Aubrey finished munching on a handful of fries. "Admit it, Miss Dailey, you haven't wanted anything to do with the shaggy-haired boy for two years. You've been talking about heading off to the city to make your fame and fortune."

"Not fame and fortune," Tabitha objected. "I just want a job that'll pay for my rent and cover my expenses, one that isn't in this small town, where I'm working for my father my whole life."

Maggie set her plate on her lap. "Is it that you really want to go to the city or that you don't want to be under your father's thumb the way you have been? There's a difference."

Tabitha rolled her eyes. There was a difference, and she hadn't even realized it until she'd started collaborating on the graphic novel project with Wes. "More getting out from under my father's thumb, but how will that happen if I still live here in town?"

"If someone loved you enough to marry you, they'd stand up to your father for you, as well," Kayla suggested.

Tabitha lifted herself from her chair and leaned against the railing to take in the New River. Wesley's view was similar, only in a more rustic part of the valley. "Or I suppose I could get a backbone and let my father know how I feel. I just hate disappointing him."

Her friends surrounded her in a group hug. She loved them and never wanted to be without them, which she would be if she ran off to the city. In the time she'd been discussing the stories of Tempus Elgato and other sci-fi/fantasy work, she'd felt invigorated. The collaboration was just the icing on the cake. Could she be happy staying in Prescott Hill if she at least had her writing to look forward to?

Who was she kidding? It wasn't just her writing that she got excited about. It was working and seeing Wesley every day. Being with him, hearing his laughter, getting breathless when he bumped into her side or took her hand. It had only been a day since she'd last spent time with him, and she was already in withdrawals.

"What is going on in that mind of yours, Miss Dailey?" Aubrey asked in between pizza bites. "I can see the wheels turning from here."

"Thinking about Wesley."

"What about Wesley?" Maggie asked.

"How much fun we have together and how much we have in common."

Kayla nodded. "That's a good thing."

"He's a good thing. He helped me see my worth as a writer and has encouraged me to pursue it more. He understands it's a passion of mine and how much enjoyment I get from it. He's helped me brainstorm ideas on how to publish this new graphic novel we've been working on and wants us to succeed. Now, I see it's not because he wanted to get rich. I assured him most writers don't make much money."

"How do you feel about Wesley, sweetie?" Maggie asked, her face concerned.

Tabitha took a deep breath in, then released it slowly. "I'm in love with him."

Aubrey perked up. "With the shaggy-haired boy you fought so hard to avoid? Quite a switch from earlier this year."

"The past two years," Kayla added.

"I know." Tabitha dropped back into her chair and covered her face with her hands. Maggie rubbed her back.

"You fought it so long because you wanted to leave town."

Tabitha's head popped up. "He does something to me, makes me feel things I didn't want to feel. Not when I had plans to blow this clambake. I knew, if I allowed him to get inside my heart, I'd be stuck here forever. Like my mother. She'd had so many dreams, and I hated to see her pining for them. I didn't want to follow in her footsteps in that way."

"I don't think Wesley will let you toss your dreams away." Kayla mimicked throwing something away. "He's got a vested interest now that he's doing the sketches for your book."

"Honestly, I think he's doing that more for me. That's not to say that he doesn't enjoy drawing and working with me, but he was satisfied to simply have his drawings there to look at. He doesn't need validation for his talent like I do. Granted, I can hardly go around telling people about my stories."

"Why can't you?" Aubrey demanded, her voice stronger than usual.

"My father wouldn't approve."

Maggie stamped her foot. "You're twenty-eight years old, Tabitha Dailey. You don't need your father's approval. Nothing you've ever done is scandalous or immoral. You need to stop beating yourself up over it."

Tabitha remembered her list of the Seven Deadly Sins and how she'd worked her way through all of them. But wanting a piece of pie was hardly something sinful. There were far worse things than buying a new hat. And every now and then she deserved to sit around and not worry about work or any of the other jobs she had to do at church and around her father's house.

"All of you are right. I'm ridiculous for getting mad at him for what he did. Of course, now he probably thinks I'm a nutcase and will want to avoid me at all costs."

"That man loves you, Tabitha," Kayla said. "He has for a few years. I'm surprised he hasn't told you yet."

"He told me he cares about me a lot. Maybe he knows I wasn't ready for the L word."

"Does that mean now you are?" Maggie asked.

"I guess, if I love him, then I want him to love me back. That's kind of how it works, isn't it?"

Aubrey frowned. "That's how it's supposed to work. It doesn't always."

Tabitha felt terrible. Here she was complaining when she had people who loved her, her father included, and poor Aubrey had missed that luxury, though she had her friends. They all loved and supported each other.

"What do I do? Should I go over there now?"

Kayla glanced at her watch. "You need to stay here and eat pizza with your best friends. He can wait. As much as I don't think he did anything wrong, I also think men shouldn't get used to instant gratification. Learning how to wait isn't a bad thing."

The others agreed, and Tabitha relaxed back into her chair. Yet when she thought of discussing the situation with Wesley, she was anything but relaxed. What if he didn't love her? Could he grow to love her? The way she loved him? What if he was so annoyed at her behavior he didn't want to even try anymore?

She couldn't think that way. The girls were right. Wesley had been showing his interest for years. In the past five months, they'd finally found some common ground and truly become friends. Perhaps more than friends.

As they watched the sun set and munched on pizza, Tabitha let her mind wander to Wesley's kisses, hoping they wouldn't be the last she'd ever get from him.

Chapter Twenty-Nine

Wesley waited until Reverend Dailey and Mrs. Chavez drove away to their meeting for the ladies of the Three Oaks Country Club. He took his time cleaning up his tools and materials. Most of the outer work for the addition was complete, but he'd decided to do some more to give Tabitha space throughout the day.

She'd been so angry with him Tuesday night and had completely avoided him yesterday, running errands most of the day. Today, she'd holed up in her office. However, he'd seen her peeking out her window more than a few times. Or maybe she was just making copies as that's where the copy machine was. He hoped she was checking for him. And missing him.

As he carried his toolbox back to his SUV, he smiled at Mrs. Mancini, who was walking away from the vehicle with a wink to him. Sure enough, a pie box sat on the passenger front seat. The woman was a miracle worker. When he'd explained the situation, she'd waved him out of her house and told him he'd have his pie by the time the church office closed the next day.

Taking the pie with him, he entered the church through the back door, placed the pie on a table, and headed to the restroom. Once he'd washed all the dirt and sweat from his hands and face, he retrieved the pie and marched to Tabitha's office.

She stood at her window, a frown on her face as she glanced out. Was she looking for him?

He tapped lightly on the door frame, and she jumped, then spun in his direction.

"Sorry. Didn't mean to scare you."

"No, it's fine. I didn't realize you were still here. You packed up your tools, so I assumed you went home."

"I didn't want to leave until I'd talked to you, Tabitha. I want to apologize for the other day. For not telling you sooner about my situation and my grandfather. It's something I try not to think of, but you're right. We've grown closer, and it was information you have a right to know."

Tabitha bit her bottom lip and inched closer. Progress.

"I should be the one apologizing. It's none of my business who your relatives are, and I'm sorry I acted like a shrew. I was already worked up from the fire, then to hear what you said ... It doesn't matter. I shouldn't have stormed off like I did. I hope you'll forgive me. I'm not normally so rude."

He smirked. "Just with me, huh? I should feel honored."

"You shouldn't have had to deal with my anger. It wasn't warranted."

"I want it to be your business who my family is. I want a lot more with you, Tabitha. Can you forgive me, please? Give me another chance."

"I told you—"

Wes held up the pie box. "This is for you. I hoped it would work the same or better than candy and flowers."

Her eyes narrowed. "What is it?"

"Mrs. Mancini's rhubarb pie."

Her jaw dropped as she took the box and peeked inside. "How did you get a pie from Mrs. Mancini?"

"I asked her for one."

"Why?"

Wesley shrugged. "Because you never get any at the Sunday potlucks, and I wanted you to have something you never get."

One of Tabitha's eyes closed as she tipped her head. "She just made you a rhubarb pie? What did you tell her you needed it for?"

"I told her I needed it for groveling to make you like me again."

"Oh, Wesley, I never stopped liking you."

He took the box and set it on her desk, then took her hands. "Mrs. Mancini made it happily. Said she was a sucker for true love."

Moisture filled her eyes. What did that mean? "True love?"

"Yes, I love you, Tabitha Dailey. I want to be with you and next to you until you feel the same way. I'll do whatever it takes for you to care about me the way I care about you."

She bit her bottom lip and laughed. "It won't take long. I already do."

Relief swept through him, and his shoulders loosened. "You do? Already? We've only been on a few dates."

Her eyes sparkled. "Did you only fall in love with me once we officially started dating?"

"No. I've been in love with you since I first met you. You are an incredible woman. I couldn't get you out of my mind."

"I've been in love with you for a while, too, Wesley. I just fought it tooth and nail because I didn't want it to happen. I was so afraid of being stuck here like my mother was."

Wes kissed her hands. "I'm happy to take you exploring all over this country, heck all over this world. You know I've got the funds for it. It'll have to be after I finish the addition because I don't shirk my obligations. But then we can go. Anywhere you want."

Her eyebrows slid together. "I can't just pick up and travel the world. That's downright decadent. What would people think?"

"Why not? I have the money, and you can use the opportunity to write. Use it as research. You've never been outside of Virginia, so everything will be new and exciting for you. We can start with this country, and once we've seen it all, we can travel abroad."

"You're tempting me too much. It all sounds wonderful, but how can I leave my father?"

"You said yourself Mrs. Chavez has the office routine down pat. Besides, we don't have to leave this minute. I do have at least another two months of the addition before it's ready. Then, I'll be happy to introduce you to all the different cultures the world has to offer. It might give you ideas for new worlds you can create for Tempus to write about."

"This is all too much to think about."

"Don't think about it too much. We still have some time. Use that time to get Mrs. Chavez completely self-sufficient in your job. Once she's indispensable, your father won't have a reason to keep you here. We could even go to Tunisia where they filmed some of the Star Wars movies. How'd you like to see that?"

Her eyes couldn't get any bigger, and he reveled in her surprise. "Oh, my word, that would be incredible."

"You are incredible. I love you so much."

"I love you, too, Wesley. You're boggling my mind right now."

"Well, while I'm scrambling your brain, I'd also like you to think about perhaps settling down in Prescott Hill, once you've done some traveling."

Her mouth tipped up at the edges. "Would you be settling down here with me?"

He framed her face and stroked her cheek with his thumb. "Oh, I most definitely hope so."

Tabitha smiled as most of the congregation patted Wesley on the back and shook his hand. The addition had finally been finished, connected to the original part of the church, and the new pews added. The Sinclair and Prescott families had wanted new pews but insisted their old name plates be moved from the rows that were now farther back.

The new front row pews had built in cushions, glove holders, and extra leg room. Her father was hoping the weekly offerings from these families would increase.

Tabitha meandered around the pavilion, picking up empty plates and cups and tossing them in the trash. They'd held Sunday service out here several weeks in a row while Wesley and his crew did the last touches on the addition. Today, the new addition had been open for all to see and use. The potluck afterward had been an extremely festive affair.

Mrs. Mancini strolled past and patted her arm. "Did you get some of my pie today?"

"I did. Wesley saved me a piece. It's just too delicious. Thank you."

"I've seen the two of you together quite often lately, so I'll assume the pie he got from me a few months ago worked its magic."

Tabitha couldn't hold back the grin. "Worked better than any flowers or candy. I appreciate how quickly you got that to him."

"How could I refuse when he said it was a matter of true love? I've seen the way he looks at you, sweetie. The way he's looked at you for years now. I've also seen the sly glances you sent his way when you thought no one was aware. I figured a rhubarb pie was the least I could do."

"No one was supposed to see the way I looked back at him. Luckily, I came to my senses and decided to give him a chance. He's definitely worth it."

Mrs. Mancini peered over her shoulder to where Cissy Hanson was preening in front of Wesley with her daughter, Carissa. Tabitha frowned.

"Now, don't you worry none, young missy. Cissy's been parading her daughter in front of eligible men for years. I'm convinced Carissa has her own paramour somewhere, but it isn't anyone her mother has introduced her to. Let's see if I can get the rest of these people out of here, so you and your young man can make some plans. He's got an anxious expression on his face."

"Thank you, Mrs. Mancini. I appreciate it."

As the woman shuffled off, waving people to their cars, Tabitha pivoted toward Wesley again. Seems she was always seeking him out. In the past two months, they'd grown infinitely closer, and they hoped to speak to her father soon. Today, if possible. Since the addition was officially finished, Wes had nothing keeping him working at the church.

It took another fifty minutes before all of the congregation had wandered home, and Wesley found his way to her.

"Where'd my father go? We were going to speak to him today, right?"

It was time to put her big girl panties on and stand up for herself. But Wesley had insisted he be right by her side while she did. In case she needed moral support.

They found her father in his office, sitting behind his desk, smiling at a small piece of paper. When they entered, he peered up, his eyes curious.

"Nicely done, Mr. Roberts. I knew I chose the right man for the job. Our little chapel on the hill is now slightly larger. Much more room for new worshipers to join us."

"Thank you, sir. I appreciate the confidence in me. It was my absolute pleasure to give this to the community."

Her father glanced back and forth between them. He hadn't said much about the fact they were dating, especially since she came home every night to her own bed.

"Dad. We wanted to talk to you about something." Tabitha clenched Wesley's hand tighter, needing courage for this discussion.

"Of course. Of course. What's on your mind?" He trained his gaze on Wesley, and Tabitha gritted her teeth. Why did he think what Wes had to say was more important than what she had to say?

Wes simply tilted his head toward her. She could do this.

"Dad, we need to hire a new church secretary."

"Church secretary? That's your position. Are you giving yourself a promotion?" He laughed at his small joke.

"No, I'm stepping down from my job. Mrs. Chavez has been here for over four months and is capable of doing every job I've done for the past ten years. I suggest you offer her the position. I'm more than willing to stay for a few more weeks to help with any transitioning."

The reverend's mouth flatlined. "What is your new job?"

She tried to get it out, but her mouth wouldn't function. Wes took the opportunity to jump in. "Tabitha is going to concentrate on her writing. She's very talented."

Her father scowled. "What writing are you talking about? How can you afford to live on that? Do you even have anything written yet?"

"She'll be living with me." The deep tone of Wesley's voice filled her with joy.

Her father's head whipped up. "What? Living together?"

"As my wife," Wes continued.

"Your wife? You just started dating a few months ago."

"True, but I've been in love with Tabitha since I first saw her. Your daughter is an extraordinary woman, sir. I'm surprised you haven't been fighting them off with a stick."

Her father gazed her way. "Tabitha?"

Squeezing his hand, she said, "I avoided Wesley because he made me feel things I didn't want to feel, conjured up emotions I wasn't ready to have yet. But they're all good things, and one of them is love."

Wesley took a half step closer to the desk. "I can afford for her not to work another job so she can focus on her writing."

"Doing additions is that lucrative?"

Wes stilled, and she knew he'd be pulling his big secret out of the bag any moment now.

"I've got a trust fund through my grandmother. It's more than enough to get me through a few lifetimes if I don't live extravagantly. Of course, I don't plan to stop working and just live off it."

"What is this writing you're talking about? When have you been a writer, Tabby Cat?"

Tabitha sighed. "I've been writing science fiction and action-adventure stories for a while now. I've sold quite a few of them to a science fiction magazine. People love them."

"She's really good," Wes added.

"Why didn't you tell me?" She'd almost guess her father was hurt, but that couldn't be right. He'd hated anything to do with fantasy as a kid. Time to grow a backbone.

"Because you scolded me any time I wanted to read or watch anything even remotely similar."

The scowl on her father's face was familiar. She knew what was coming.

"Listen, reverend, sir. I love Tabitha, and I want her to be happy. She gets such joy from writing and using her imagination to create these marvelous worlds. If you're going to treat her poorly like she's done something wrong or make her feel guilty for doing something that is perfectly respectable, we'll move somewhere else. I love Prescott Hill and the people in it, but I love Tabitha more."

Her father paused and glanced between the two of them as they stood there, wondering what he was thinking. "This is what you want, Tabby Cat?"

"I was planning to leave town as soon as I'd saved up enough money to live on in the city. Probably in the next few months."

"You'd just up and leave me?"

Her courage was bolstered by the man at her side. "I don't enjoy being a church secretary. I've done it for so long to help you, but it's never been my dream. I don't want to give up my dreams like mom did. She always loved drawing and painting. She rarely got to do that once she got married and had to do her duty as pastor's wife."

Her father nodded, and a sad expression crossed his face. "Your mother was very talented. Her face used to light up when she was sketching or painting. I didn't realize she was unhappy."

"She wasn't, Dad. She loved you and me and all the people in town, but she would have been more fulfilled if she'd been able to create her art alongside serving the parishioners."

"I don't want you to be miserable, Tabby Cat, and I certainly don't want you to leave town. I'd miss you terribly. What exactly is it you want?"

"First and foremost, I want to marry Wesley. We love each other and want to be together. I want to be able to write the stories I love and not have to hide it, as well as be able to wear clothes and do things I like to do without feeling I've let you down. I don't plan to suddenly start wearing anything skimpy or go on all night drinking binges, but I want to have fun, by myself, without always feeling like I'm the preacher's daughter. I won't embarrass you, Dad, but I can't continue under the oppressive rules I've lived by all my life. I'm twenty-eight years old. I need to make my own decisions and my own mistakes."

Her father sighed. "I guess I sometimes forget how grown up you are. You'll always be my little girl. I'm sorry I didn't realize you felt this way. Be assured you've never done anything that embarrassed me. I'm just so used to guiding my sheep that I forget you always knew exactly where you were and didn't need any guiding."

Wes curled his arm around her shoulder. "I'll take over the guiding for you, so you can concentrate on your lost ones. I don't think I'll need to do that much, anyway. More likely, Tabitha will be the one to guide me, to make sure I do everything possible so she's happy."

Her father stood, one eyebrow crooked. "See that you do, or you'll get one of my fire and brimstone sermons up close and personal."

Epilogue

Wesley gazed down at the beautiful woman in front of him, declaring her love yet again. They'd done it in the chapel a short while ago, and now he had her in his arms, swirling her around the dance floor.

"I love you, too, Mrs. Roberts. Thank you for taking a chance on me."

Tabitha's smile warmed his heart, and he hoped he'd be able to keep it there forever.

"Thank you for not giving up on me when I gave you so many reasons to walk away. I'm glad you didn't."

He pressed a quick kiss to her lips. "I couldn't. It would be like walking away from my heart. I wouldn't be able to survive."

Her smile grew. "Such a romantic. No wonder I fell in love with you. That and your adorable grin."

He threw that grin her way, and she blushed. He loved how easily her pale skin showed color. The song ended and a fast one began. Before they could get grooving, Kayla waved them over.

Aubrey, Maggie, and Donovan stood beside Kayla.

"We're so thrilled you two finally got together," Kayla said, embracing both Wes and Tabitha.

"And that you decided to have the wedding in the same barn Donovan and I did." Maggie glanced around at the gaily decorated space.

"I hope it's what you wanted." Aubrey seemed nervous, having been the one to coordinate the decor.

"I love it, Aubrey. You've got such a knack for this." Tabitha waved at the venue.

Wesley tipped his chin at Donovan and Maggie. "Have you ever considered turning this place into a wedding venue? It's been used twice now. It would bring in extra income."

"I don't have time to do that on top of running the farm," Maggie replied.

Tabitha bit her lip. "Maybe Aubrey could run it. Look at what she's done to this place."

Aubrey's eyes widened in excitement. "It's been fun sprucing the barn up for both your weddings."

Maggie hugged her husband's arm. "Maybe we'll consider it. It's kind of a lot for one person to undertake. Not to mention the money you'd need to get a business started."

Donovan narrowed his eyes and peered skyward. "You know, my cousin Travis was talking about investing in a start-up business closer to Prescott Hill. I'll mention it to him. This area could use a good function hall that isn't stuffy like the country club."

Kayla lifted her shoulders and laughed. "That would be wonderful. Having your wedding at a rustic building in a beautiful rural location is all the rage these days. If you teamed up with the Prescott Inn to house the guests and the wedding party, plus maybe do the catering, it could be a win win situation."

Aubrey gave a discreet cough. "Perhaps a local baker, like Mrs. Barrios, could be persuaded to make cakes or other desserts. Add in a photographer and you'd have pretty much everything in a one-stop shop kind of deal."

Donovan tipped his head. "So, Aubrey, would you be interested in taking on something like that? I can certainly mention it to my cousin and see what he says."

Aubrey winced. "Is that your stuffy cousin who I was partnered with at your wedding?"

"Yes." Maggie rolled her eyes. "He's actually a pretty nice guy. I think my mother-in-law was giving him a hard time about stuff that day, so he might not have been in the best mood."

"I suppose I could give him the benefit of the doubt. If he even wants to discuss the possibility. Maggie, it's your barn, though. Do you want to have lots of strangers traipsing across your yard every weekend?"

"If it brings in more business for Popham Farm, absolutely. I'd have to insist that most of the food comes from our produce and animals, but Chef Dupree never has a problem using our inventory."

"Sounds like a done deal, as long as your cousin is willing to invest, Donovan," Wes said.

Donovan's gaze was across the room. "I'll talk to him. I'm wondering what the deal is with your father, Tabitha. He and Mrs. Chavez seem to be awfully cozy lately."

Wes scowled at his friend. "Awfully cozy? When did you become a girl, interested in stuff like that?"

Donovan glared back. "I've just never seen Reverend Dailey quite so relaxed."

Tabitha smiled and said, "Well, she's been working in the office now for seven months. My father can't say enough about how efficient she is."

Maggie shrugged her shoulder. "Bitsy mentioned at dinner just last week how Mrs. Chavez has gotten the reverend to attend the ladies' luncheon each week to speak on several different subjects. They all love having him there."

Kayla eyed the mature couple now slow dancing. Very properly, of course. "If that's any indication, you might need to step up plans to turn this into a wedding venue soon enough."

Tabitha watched as her father spun the woman on the dance floor. "It would be nice if my father found someone else to keep him company, especially now that I'll be moving into Wesley's place after our honeymoon."

Aubrey laughed. "Like you haven't brought most of your stuff over there already."

Tabitha made a face at her friend. "We've been perfectly proper. My clothes may have stayed there a few times, but I've been returned home to my father's every night."

"No more, though." Wes kissed his wife's nose. "My home is now our home, and that's where you'll be staying every night from now on."

Her face turned up to his, her eyes twinkling. "Except for when we travel, right? I can't wait to see the world. Discover new places and cultures. Incorporate them into my writing."

Their graphic novel had been picked up by Rory's publisher friend, and they'd delivered the last of the final drawings and text just last week. It would be another six months before the story started running in *Galaxia*, but it was all planned out between the magazine and the publisher. They'd gotten a small advance with their contract, and she'd been thrilled. He and Tabitha had already begun planning another few stories in that universe. While they traveled, they intended to outline some of them.

Tabitha had finally been able to focus on her love of writing, and Wesley had discovered his talents as an artist. How far they'd go with these books, they didn't know. But right now, they were having fun and enjoying working together. Thankfully, his trust fund was keeping the bills paid while they explored intergalactic worlds.

Mrs. Mancini ambled past and shook her finger at them. "Go and canoodle on the dance floor. It's your wedding day. You should spend it holding each other close."

Wes grinned at the older lady. "We'll be doing plenty of holding tonight, for sure."

Mrs. Mancini chuckled. "With the way you look at each other, I have a feeling you'll be holding each other close for many, many years to come."

If you liked *Tabitha: Always a Bridesmaid*, please consider leaving a review. It doesn't have to be long and reviews help other readers find new books.

TABITHA

If you want to see more of Prescott Hill (Aubrey and Kayla and maybe others...), sign up for Kari's newsletter for up-to-date information on new releases and sales.

karilemor.com

HERE'S WHERE YOU CAN FIND KARI LEMOR

Website: https://www.karilemor.com/

Facebook: https://www.facebook.com/Karilemorauthor/

The Lit Lounge — Kari's Reader Group -
https://www.facebook.com/groups/373521153021256

Last Chance Beach Romance Readers (FB) -
https://www.facebook.com/groups/290055732591791

Romance Gems Where Authors and Readers Meet (FB)-
https://www.facebook.com/groups/332592250930075

The Corner of Love and Main — small town romance reader's group
(FB) - https://www.facebook.com/groups/cornerofloveandmain

Twitter: https://twitter.com/karilemor

Instagram: https://www.instagram.com/karilemorauthor/

Pinterest: https://www.pinterest.com/karilemor/

Goodreads:
https://www.goodreads.com/author/show/9756283.Kari_Lemor

BookBub: https://www.bookbub.com/authors/kari-lemor

Made in the USA
Middletown, DE
23 January 2024

48229623R00142